ISBN 978-1-331-38242-3
PIBN 10182336

1 MONTH OF
FREE
READING

at

www.ForgottenBooks.com

By purchasing this book you are eligible for one month membership to ForgottenBooks.com, giving you unlimited access to our entire collection of over 1,000,000 titles via our web site and mobile apps.

To claim your free month visit:

www.forgottenbooks.com/free182336

English
Français
Deutsche
Italiano
Español
Português

www.forgottenbooks.com

Mythology Photography **Fiction**
Fishing Christianity **Art** Cooking
Essays Buddhism Freemasonry
Medicine **Biology** Music **Ancient
Egypt** Evolution Carpentry Physics
Dance Geology **Mathematics** Fitness
Shakespeare **Folklore** Yoga Marketing
Confidence Immortality Biographies
Poetry **Psychology** Witchcraft
Electronics Chemistry History **Law**
Accounting **Philosophy** Anthropology
Alchemy Drama Quantum Mechanics
Atheism Sexual Health **Ancient History**
Entrepreneurship Languages Sport
Paleontology Needlework Islam
Metaphysics Investment Archaeology
Parenting Statistics Criminology
Motivational

" Saved in his Eskimo suit."   *Frontispiece.*   (*See page* 247.)

SHIPWRECKED
IN
GREENLAND

BY

ARTHUR R. THOMPSON

AUTHOR OF "G—SELL—————————"

Illustrated

—OSTON

AND COMPANY

"........ his Riddam soft." *Frontispiece.* (See page 247.)

SHIPWRECKED

IN

GREENLAND

BY

ARTHUR R. THOMPSON
AUTHOR OF "GOLD-SEEKING ON THE DALTON TRAIL"

Illustrated from Photographs

BOSTON
LITTLE, BROWN, AND COMPANY
1905

THE UNIVERSITY PRESS, CAMBRIDGE, U. S. A.

TO

MY MOT·HER

THIS BOOK IS AFFECTIONATELY
DEDICATED

PREFACE

THE following story is based in part upon the experiences of that unfortunate expedition which, on board the steamer *Miranda*, came to grief off the coast of Greenland in the summer of 1894. Wherever the narrative deals with the hospitable Danish officials, or with the self-sacrificing fishermen of the Gloucester schooner *Rigel*, it has seemed fitting to retain their proper names in grateful recognition of their services.

Special courtesies during the preparation of this volume from Prof. William H. Brewer, of Yale, Prof. G. Frederick Wright, of Oberlin, Hon. James D. Dewell, of New Haven, and Mr. Rudolf Kersting, of New York, are hereby acknowledged with thanks.

ARTHUR R. THOMPSON.

CONTENTS

LIST OF ILLUSTRATIONS

SHIPWRECKED IN GREENLAND

CHAPTER I

A NEWFOUNDLAND CAMP

ABOUT thirty miles north of the city of St. John's, Newfoundland, at the extremity of the long promontory between Conception and Trinity Bays, is Breakheart Point. Were it not for the heights of Bacalieu Island a few miles out at sea, this cape would be one of the bleakest on the east coast, with nothing to mitigate the fury of the North Atlantic. As it is, Bacalieu affords some shelter, and offers as well an inviting region for exploration, being far out of the usual lines of travel. For these reasons, among others, the party of campers whose adventures are about to be related chose to locate first near Breakheart Point, intending to spend the earlier part of their outing on the coast, and the remainder by some lake or river inland. During the third week in July they had arrived, seven in number, on board Captain Robert Ayre's sloop, and had pitched two tents a little back from the grassy summit of a cliff overlooking the sea.

Two days later, at about eight o'clock in the evening, Caesar Williams might have been seen on the edge of the bluff looking fixedly seaward, his hand above his eyes. Caesar was the colored cook and handy man about the camp. For years he had been a trusted servant in the Schuyler household in New York, and though young Philip Schuyler, a stout lad of fourteen, had brought him along supposedly for no other duties than those mentioned, Mrs. Schuyler had secretly charged the faithful man to keep an eye on her son.

His observation finished, Caesar walked back to the camp-fire, scratching his gray wool thoughtfully.

"Ef dey doan git back right soon," said he to Phil, who sat on a block of driftwood near him, "I's gwine gib 'em up fo' de night. Mebbe dey gwine ter roost on Bacalieu; but I b'lieve dey ain' got no supper wid 'em, an' dere ain' no hotels out yondah. Bettah keep de food an' drink hot awhile, I reck'n."

"Yes, Caesar," answered Phil, looking up from a tangle of fishing-lines. "The wind is fair and plenty of it, so they're not becalmed, that's sure. They ought to be in sight soon, and they'll be as hungry as bears."

"Dat am what," said Caesar. "Well, I spec we

doan need ter worry 'bout 'em. Cap'n, he's a fust-rate sailorman, an' dat Malcolm boy o' his'n 'pears ter be mos' as good, — an' as fer Marse Henry, he know 'bout eberyt'ing. Ef 't was us four lan'lubbers now, gone off in dat sloop, 't would be a heap mo' decomposin' to de mind. Whar 'd Ralph an' Andy make off wid demselves to?"

"They went after firewood, I think," answered Phil.

Two young fellows scrambled up a slope behind the tents as he spoke. Each carried a section of a small log on his shoulder, and one had an axe in his free hand. Quickly throwing their loads down close to the fire, they cast a glance of inquiry around the camp.

"Have n't they come yet?" asked the elder, a well-knit youth of seventeen, with light hair, blue eyes, and a number of honest freckles.

"No, Andy," replied Phil. "Caesar's just been to the cliff and could n't see a sign of them. Where 'd you find your tree?"

"We had to go back about a mile. There's nothing but scrubby stuff near the salt water."

"That's the only trouble with this camping place," put in Ralph, his companion. "Good timber's going to be hard to reach, and most of the driftwood is too wet to burn. I don't want to carry any more logs across such a rough country. Can't we dry out some driftwood around the fire?"

"Dat we can," declared Caesar. "Phil, ef yo' 'll rise up offen dat piece I 'll put it whar de water 'll des sizzle out of it. Yo' ain' never goin' ter dry it sittin' on it."

Phil jumped up, and after winding the fish-line around a stick he proposed that they all go down to the cove and bring up a good supply of the driftwood. The others assented, and the four set off to the shore of a small inlet where some water-logged wreckage had collected. At the end of half an hour as much of this had been secured as could be conveniently disposed about the fire. In the meantime Ralph had spied the belated sloop rounding the northern end of Bacalieu, — for in that latitude the summer daylight lasts well into the night.

When the three navigators reached the camp, having moored their craft in the lee of the rocks, the fire had been piled high, and Caesar was ready to welcome them with hot biscuits and tea and bacon and fried potatoes.

Captain Ayre threw his sou'wester and oilskin coat into the larger tent, and sat down with a look of keen anticipation to the improvised table whereon the good things were spread. He was a big, hearty man, with ruddy face and a short beard sprinkled with gray. His son Malcolm, an active young fellow of eighteen, was soon beside him, followed presently by Henry Hollister.

Marse Henry, as Caesar always called him, had recently graduated from the Sheffield Scientific School as a civil 'engineer. He and Ralph were brothers. The latter, aged sixteen, was a student in a Connecticut high school, with hopes of entering college in two or three years. He was slender, but wiry and enduring. Henry was of a decidedly athletic build, and had been captain of a winning crew while in the University. His features, though partly concealed by a closely trimmed brown beard, indicated firmness and ability to command. The summer outing was of his devising, and his qualities as well as his age had made him the acknowledged leader of the party from the day on which they left New York for St. John's on the steamer Portia.

Andrew Faxon and Philip Schuyler were cousins of the Hollister brothers. Andy, during all his seventeen years, had lived on a prairie farm in Nebraska, and though he had read marvellous tales of the ocean, he had longed in vain to see it. Hence

he accepted the more eagerly the invitation of his
Connecticut relatives to share their fortunes for
the summer.

Henry had selected his companions with care.
Each was chosen on account of certain qualities or
abilities which would contribute to the interests and
pleasure of all. For instance, Ralph, his younger
brother, was very observing and an eager student
of botany and geology, — in fact, an embryo nat-
uralist, and full of profitable information. Andy
brought much useful knowledge of camping and
a country-bred capacity for accomplishing things.
Being of a practical and cautious turn of mind, he
acted as a sort of check upon the youngster Philip,
who was inclined to be hasty and impulsive. Philip's
specialty was photography. Caesar's usefulness was
multitudinous. As for Captain Ayre and Malcolm,
they had been enlisted at St. John's with their sloop
in order that it might be possible to make short trips
along the coast for hunting, fishing, and exploration.
Two more genial and capable sailors could not have
been found in Newfoundland.

The services of the Ayres were secured through
a fortunate combination of circumstances. The Captain was commander and part owner of a sealing
steamer, the Great Auk. Each spring, when the ice-

floes moved southward along the shores of Labrador
and Newfoundland, he took his vessel out with the
rest of the St. John's fleet and pushed into the ice
wherever the seals were plentiful. The voyage of
the present season being over, the Great Auk had
been placed in the dry-dock for painting and repairs,
and the presence of neither the Captain nor Malcolm
would be needed through the summer.

Malcolm had accompanied his father on several
sealing trips, and had shown a natural aptitude for
navigation. He owned a half-interest in the sloop,
which was appropriately named Little Auk, and
could handle her in any kind of weather.

No sooner had the Captain and Henry and Malcolm seated themselves at the table on little rustic
chairs contrived by Andy, than the others crowded
around, eager to hear about their voyage.

"You must have caught a lot of fish," said Phil,
like an ant putting out a feeler.

"No, we did n't keep at it very long," replied
Henry. "We hauled in six or eight cod this morning, — enough to supply us for a few days, — and
then pulled in our lines. You 'll find the cod down
there in the sloop."

"What could have delayed you, then?" persisted
Phil. "Anybody 'd think you had some news up

your sleeves — you three. What in the world have you been up to?"

"Ah!" said Captain Ayre, with a mysterious smile, "that's a question we're in doubt about answering. Fact is, we made a discovery, and can't quite decide what effect it's going to have on this encampment. We don't like to disappoint you boys."

Ralph noticed traces of a smile about the corners of the Captain's mouth and concluded that they were not likely to be disappointed.

"In what way?" he ventured to ask.

"I leave it to Mr. Hollister," said the Captain. "He's in command, and if he's willing to tell you, why, all right."

The worthy skipper, having thus washed his hands of all responsibility, proceeded to stow away Caesar's provisions at a wonderful rate. But he had said enough to set in motion the curiosity of his youngest hearers, and Henry saw that there would be no stemming the tide. Being at once appealed to by Andy and Ralph and Phil together, he said, after a moment's thought, "We may have to pull up stakes."

"And go home?" asked Phil, with a rueful face.

"No, but change our plans and give up camping for the present. Our future course, if changed, will involve hard work and undoubtedly some risk. It's the risk that makes me hesitate. I don't know that I ought to ask any of you to undertake a dangerous mission."

Andy gave expression to his feelings by a low whistle. "Do tell us what you 've discovered," he pleaded presently. "If I were back in Nebraska I should say it could n't be anything less startling than the last surviving buffalo, but around here I don't know what to expect."

"If you did, it would n't help you much, Andy," declared Malcolm. "It 's about the last thing any one would think of, and the biggest piece of luck I ever saw. Why, everything on board was —" he checked himself, feeling that the elder Hollister should be the spokesman.

"I 'll tell you," said Henry. "We found a large steamer drifting just east of Bacalieu Island. Everything indicated that she had been hurriedly abandoned. There was not a soul on board, and we took possession."

"Fo' de lan' sakes!" said Caesar, who had listened open-mouthed.

CHAPTER II

THE MYSTERIOUS STEAMER

HENRY would have preferred to keep this exciting news until the next morning, partly because he did not wish to have the boys lying awake half the night, and partly because he desired time enough for deciding independently upon a course of action. But he had not taken the precaution of warning the Captain and Malcolm. Now that the secret was out he could only advise his fellow campers to try to get a full night's rest, since they might need all their energies on the morrow, and he promised to call a council immediately after breakfast, when the whole subject would be thoroughly discussed. Further than this he would say nothing, but set a good example by turning in at once.

Philip was not to be put off too easily. He thirsted for delightful adventures on board the strange craft, and tried to elicit further information from Malcolm. That young sailor was wary and referred him back to Henry. The Captain was also

non-committal when Ralph and Phil together be-
sieged him. So at length Henry's advice was
accepted, and the camp became quiet, except an occasional crackling of the fire and snores from the
store-tent, which was Caesar's domain.

All were up early next morning and breakfasted
in haste. Then Henry, as he had agreed, called
his council to order. The seven seated themselves
close around the fire, for a dense and chill fog had
crept in from the sea during the night, and as yet
the sun had made little impression upon it.

" I 'm going to tell you briefly what we did yesterday," Henry began, " and explain the situation
as well as I can. Then we 'll talk it over and see
what we ought to do.

" We set out, as you know, to explore some parts
of Bacalieu, and also to try the fishing near the
island. We landed several times during the morning without seeing much but rocks, a few berries,
and some stunted vegetation. Then we re-embarked
and caught those cod. I suggested that we sail into
the narrow strait that, divides the island into two
parts from north to south, for it is said to be exceedingly picturesque, with towering walls, on the
ledges of which cling a few small houses of fishermen. But the wind was so light that the Captain

feared we should be becalmed in there, so we continued around the northern end, meantime eating
the dinner which Caesar had provided. The Captain
and Malcolm wished to show me the great cliffs
where millions of sea-birds have their nests.

"We were getting well to the eastward of the
island, where heavy mists were just breaking, when
the Captain sighted a steamer close inshore in a
little bay. Her position was so unusual that he remarked upon it. She did not seem to be moving,
and so far as we could judge was either anchored or
aground. No smoke rose from her funnel, nor could
we see anything of her people on the deck or the
nearest shore.

"'There's something queer about this,' says the
Captain. 'I think we'd better investigate.'

"So we made as straight for the steamer as the
wind would let us, and soon we could read the name
Viola on her bow. Still there was no one to be seen,
and that struck us as very curious. We hailed her
then, but no sound followed except the echoes from
the cliffs, which at first we mistook for an answer.
So, running alongside, we lowered sail and made
fast to the port ladder.

"Malcolm went up first, then the Captain and I.
We examined the decks quickly, and finding nothing

unusual there we passed down the companionway and through the dining-saloon, the engine-room, and such parts of the hold and forecastle as we could easily reach, not forgetting to make a hasty search of the staterooms. Having satisfied ourselves that there was no one on board, we returned to the deck, where Captain Ayre ascertained that the ship was neither anchored nor aground. The wind was blowing gently in from the sea, and the Viola was slowly but surely drifting toward the cliffs."

" Ef dat wa'n't a pity," broke in Caesar. " Did she hit on de rocks ? "

Henry had no mind to have his story pushed along too fast, and merely shook his head.

" My first thought," he continued, " was to drop one of the anchors, but the Captain doubted if it would reach bottom in that spot. So, at his suggestion, we launched a lifeboat and rowed ashore with a line from the bow, making it fast around a big boulder. Then we carried another line from the stern to the opposite side of the bay, thus bringing her to a stand. Having cared for the steamer, we went ashore, climbed the cliffs, and set off in separate directions to search for the passengers and crew. This was a forlorn hope, since we had found all the boats in their places, and we had to return without discovering so much as a footprint. We conjectured that the Viola had drifted toward the coast in the darkness of the night and the fog of the morning, and that her people had been taken off elsewhere by some other vessel. What we could not explain was the fact of the abandonment, for the ship appeared to be in perfect order."

"How large a steamer is she?" asked Andy.

"As to that," replied Henry, "Captain Ayre can answer much better than I."

The Captain reflected a moment. "I should estimate she might be a vessel of eleven hundred tons. She hails from Liverpool, — we read that on her stern. I think she's properly a freight steamer. There are, however, some extra staterooms forward which look new. Possibly she had been chartered for some special cruise. She might stow sixty passengers quite comfortably."

"What are we going to do with her?" Phil asked.

"I was coming to that," said Henry. "Probably you all know that if we could bring her into port we could claim the salvage. On a steamer as large as the Viola the salvage allowed by law would be a very considerable sum. Evidently her presence on this coast was not known before we found her, but she may be sighted from a passing ship or from the island at any moment if the weather clears. This fog is the luckiest thing in the world. Now the question is, can we seven take the Viola down to St. John's? If so, the entire salvage is ours. On the other hand, as the Captain has told me, we should need a larger crew in case of a severe storm, and need it badly. If all of us felt well and the weather favored there would be a fair chance of success, but it means the hardest kind of work, and that was n't what you came here for. Now let's hear from each one, and first from you, Captain Ayre."

" There would n't be any question in my mind," said that mariner, " if I had a regular crew. Such a steamer would carry from twenty-five to thirty-five able-bodied men, according to the service she was engaged in. She would n't carry the larger number unless there were a good many passengers. In the present case there would be none, and a crew of twenty to twenty-five would be about right."

" Just tell us, Captain, as you told me yesterday, how many men would be needed for the various duties," suggested Henry.

" Certainly. There would be a captain, first officer or mate, and second officer. That's three. Chief engineer, second engineer, and probably a third. Then the boatswain, carpenter, cook — "

" Dat 's me ! " broke in Caesar, enthusiastically.

" Sure enough, Caesar," said the Captain, laughing. " And you 'd want an assistant, no doubt, if you should cook for a whole crew."

" Yas, suh, but not fo' dis crew."

" What if you got seasick ? " asked Ralph.

" Huh ! Ef I done got seasick I reck'n dar 'ud be mo' ob de same stripe. I ain' gwine lose no sleep ober dat."

This provoked a merry shout. Caesar's argument was irrefutable, however, and the Captain proceeded to say that the remainder of the crew would consist of seamen and stokers in about equal numbers.

" But it 's true, is it not, that some of the seamen could be dispensed with if there were no cargo to handle ? " inquired Henry.

" Yes," said the Captain, " but you must have enough to stand watch, tend the wheel, and take care of things generally, — four or five at the very least."

" But supposing the decks were n't washed down and the brasses were n't polished and the man at the wheel acted as lookout ? "

" Why, then you might do with two if you worked them hard enough; but it would n't be a tidy craft that you 'd bring into port." The Captain looked distressed at the very thought.

" This is a case of necessity," said Henry. " I 'm
trying to cut down the number to a sort of prize crew,
such as they put upon a captured ship in time of war.
How about the stokers, Captain ? "

" It would be hard to reduce them much, — but
say five."

" Then we 've a crew of seven already, without
any officers. It looks rather hopeless on the surface."

" Could n't we get some of the Bacalieu fishermen
to help us ? " asked Andy.

" Yes, if necessary," Henry answered; " but it
would be something of an exploit to do the job ourselves. Even at slow speed in the fog we could probably make St. John's in half a day. The Captain
and Malcolm and I talked the matter over pretty
thoroughly on the way back yesterday, and we came
to the conclusion that it would be a comparatively
safe venture if the weather held good. But I want
you to see from the Captain's remarks that there 's
more than one man's work for each of us. The ship
appears to be stanch and seaworthy, and we should
examine her still more carefully before moving her.
The effective strength and quality of our crew I figure
out like this. Captain Ayre is as competent to command and navigate this steamer as he is to command
and navigate his own. For so short a voyage he can

be both steersman and lookout, leaving Malcolm free
for such duties as might fall to the mate and boatswain.   Andy and Ralph and Phil, with the occasional assistance of Malcolm and Caesar, will have
to do the stoking.   Caesar will cook, and I will act
as engineer, — first, second, and third.   In case of
need we can help one another to some extent in any
part of the ship.   Now you have the matter before
you, and I will call for the opinion of each one.
Captain Ayre, what is yours ? "

"I am willing to try," said the Captain, briefly.

"Malcolm, are you of the same mind ? "

"You can count on me every time, sir."

"Andy ? "

"I don't know the least thing about ships and
stoking," said Andy, dubiously, "but I'll be only
too glad to do the best I can."

"You're ingenious, Andy, and it won't take you
long to learn.   We'll make a sailor of you, and a
stoker too, in no time.   Ralph, do you wish to go
home ? "

"Pooh ! " said Ralph, quite disgusted, though he
knew his brother was joking.   "What do you think
I'm made of ? "

"What do you say, Phil ?   Are you willing to soil
those white hands ? "

" It 's the biggest kind of a lark," answered that youth, promptly. " I 'll shovel coal or do anything."

" Very good. Caesar, I believe, has already assumed the office of cook, so it seems to be unanimously voted that we take the Viola to St. John's. I did n't wish to reach this decision hastily, but now that it 's made we 've not a moment to lose. Down with the tents, boys. We must take everything on board the sloop at once."

" Jes' one word, Marse Henry," said Caesar, as the four lads rushed excitedly for the tents. " Is yo' quite sartin dat dere kyarn't no harm come to young Phil ? "

" I 'm sure he 'll be safe if he travels with you, Caesar. We 'll all look out for him too."

The Captain and his son disappeared in the direction of the cove to make ready the sloop, while the others soon struck the tents and neatly folded them. Inside of half an hour the whole camping equipment had been carried to the water's edge and safely stowed on the deck and in the cabin of the Little Auk. A light east wind just ruffled the surface of the dull green sea. The fog was still as thick as ever, and each member of the party wore a suit of yellow oilskin as a protection against the dampness. Phil would have liked to photograph the sloop and her picturesque crew as she glided out of the cove, but time was too precious even had the light permitted.

" There 's one thing I 'm sorry I could n't do before we embarked," said Henry, as the sail caught the breeze outside the little bay and the shore disappeared in the grayness.

" What 's that ? " asked Phil.

" If there had been any opportunity I should have sent a letter home with at least a hint of this change in our plans. It is conceivable that we might be delayed in one way or another, and not a soul on shore would know where we had gone. It would be a most mysterious affair if we did n't turn up at St. John's pretty soon."

" I guess there 'll be a sensation when we do," remarked Ralph.

In due course the Little Auk beat her way around to the east side of Bacalieu Island, and as she crept down the coast the mists began to lift and the sun struggled through the rifts. These signs of clear weather were noted with dismay, but there was no help for it. The Viola was moored at an unfrequented part of the shore, and she might escape observation for some time yet.

" The first thing to do when we reach the steamer," said Henry, " will be to make a more systematic search of her than we could do yesterday. This search and everything pertaining to navigation and the duties of the crew will be as Captain Ayre orders. We must all obey him implicitly. How would it do, Captain, to give us instructions now with regard to the search?"

"A good idea," replied the Captain. "I will ask you then, Mr. Hollister, to examine the engines very carefully, and get them oiled and in working order."

"Ay, ay, sir," said Henry, after the manner of an old salt.

"Caesar, you will get as familiar as you can with the galley and all the cooking gear, and don't forget that we shall want a meal somewhere about noon."

"I 'll see to dat, sho' nuff," was Caesar's prompt reply.

"Andy and Phil will take a look through the hold and see what cargo there is, if any, and keep an eye open for some clue to the port of departure and the destination of the Viola. Ralph and Malcolm will go through the staterooms and also try to throw light on this mystery. In the meantime," concluded the Captain, "I will estimate the amount of coal on board, and examine the boilers, steering gear, pilot-house, and forecastle. All hands can report to me at noon."

CHAPTER III

CAPTAIN AYRE MAKES A DISCOVERY

THE Viola was found undisturbed in the little bay. Beyond, along the sides of the dark cliffs, trailed the mists which had effectually hidden her in the absence of her discoverers. The three younger lads and Caesar were quite astonished at her size, for they had obtained a very vague idea from the Captain's description. The thought of taking possession of this fine ship filled them with enthusiastic anticipations, and they scrambled up the ladder with more haste than ceremony, their voices starting the sea-fowl from the rocks till hundreds were circling about them.

Once on board, each member of the party set off for his appointed place. The shouts and exclamations of the younger ones suddenly ceased, for it was so very still below decks. The silence there was uncanny. It seemed as if the ghosts of the missing passengers and crew might be lurking somewhere about, and every door was opened by the explorers slowly and with caution. Their words came in whispers, and they found themselves unconsciously walking on tiptoe. Andy and Phil did not know the way to the hold till Malcolm pointed out a passageway leading to an iron-bound door.

"That'll take you to the after-hold," said he; "and here's a lantern, Andy, which you may need. Be mighty careful of it, lad. There are other compartments forward, but you'd probably have to enter them from the deck through the hatchways. If they're closed I'll help you later."

While the search was in progress Caesar unloaded such provisions as he needed from the sloop, and soon had the galley fire going. Appetizing odors presently permeated the ship and aided in dispelling the air of solitude and mystery which hung about her. At the noon hour a big dinner-bell summoned all hands to the saloon, where the middle one of three long tables was laid with the ship's china. A substantial meal had been prepared of soup, canned corned beef, potatoes, bread, pudding, coffee, and other good things.

"You've done some exploring yourself, haven't you, Caesar?" said Henry, as he took his seat. "That cheese and those crackers didn't come from our supplies."

"Dat's so, suh," answered the beaming cook. "You's right, Marse Henry. An' dar's a few mo' delic'sies fo' de dessert what ain' on de table yet."

"Good! We'll want a taste of them before long."

Noticing that the searchers were already comparing notes, Captain Ayre now suggested that the reports be heard, and called first upon Henry.

"I have examined the engines as thoroughly as the time allowed," began Henry. "They are in better shape than I expected. The engineers evidently rubbed all the exposed parts with oil before leaving. I can't account otherwise for the small amount of rust. Probably that goes to show that the steamer was not abandoned very hastily, and there was some hope of her surviving."

"The point is well taken, as a lawyer would say," observed the Captain, who was by no means an uneducated man. "That's the first link in our chain of evidence."

"I have gone over the principal working parts," continued Henry, "and see no reason why the engines can't be used. Perhaps there's no need of a more detailed story."

"I think you have given us the essential facts," said the Captain. "Now, Andy and Phil, you've been in the hold, haven't you? Andy, suppose you make the report, and Phil, you watch and see that he does n't forget anything."

"We explored only one room," said Andy. "That was the one Malcolm showed us. It was full of boxes and barrels and bags and cans and trunks, and we did n't know exactly where to begin. We decided to search the trunks first, thinking we might learn something about their owners. Those that were locked — and most of them were — we did not try to open. Several had addresses on the outside, and we made a list of these. New York, Chicago, St. Louis, Cleveland, Boston, Hartford, and Pittsburg were among the cities represented, so we feel sure the Viola started out from the United States."

"And rightly," declared the Captain. "We shall find out a good deal, I 'm thinking. Well, go on, Andy."

"We found three trunks unlocked, and ransacked them from top to bottom. They contained clothing, tools, ribbons, knives, mirrors, needles, fish-hooks, packages of tobacco, corn-cob pipes, and a lot of other small articles. We thought it was a queer assortment."

"Yes," put in Phil. "Andy was sure the owners were colonists going off somewhere to start a country store."

" It looks to me," said Henry, " as if their idea was not to start a store, but to trade from the ship with some rude tribe, — perhaps the Eskimos."

" That's just what I was on the point of saying," declared the Captain. " Ribbons and tobacco and such-like stuff are always wanted by the Huskies, as the sailors call those people. I carry some knick-knacks myself when I go sealing. Don't always have a chance to get rid of them, but sometimes we touch along the Labrador coast and pick up a few furs from the natives. Well, what next, Andy? "

" That's about all we found among the trunks," Andy went on. " Then we turned our attention to the boxes and barrels and bags. They were filled with provisions, — canned goods, vegetables, ham, bacon, hardtack, flour, and a lot more things to eat, not to mention drinkables. Most of the cases were tagged or marked with the names of wholesale pro-vision dealers in Brooklyn and New York. The dinner-bell rang just as we were leaving to go upstairs and — "

" Upstairs! " Phil laughed in spite of himself. " Oh, Andy, you certainly were brought up a long way from the ocean."

" What's the matter? " asked Andy, in aston-ishment.

" Why, there is n't any upstairs on a ship."

" Well, I saw some stairs, anyway."

" That was the companionway," said Henry. " Phil has had opportunities to learn these things on board his father's yacht, but you can give him points about the prairies, I 'll warrant. If you say you were intending to go on deck, Phil will have no ground for merriment."

" And what is it when you — when you descend ? " inquired Andy, cautiously.

" Oh, then you just go below," said Phil, eager to atone for his fun-making. " I 'll tell you how to know the time by the ship's bell, too, after dinner."

Andy declared he was willing to learn; and the Captain took advantage of the succeeding lull in the conversation to call for the report of Malcolm and Ralph on their tour of the staterooms. Malcolm began.

" We found all the doors unlocked," said he. " The rooms were in some disorder, and the berths had not been made up since they were last occupied. A good deal of the bed-clothing was missing. In the way of personal clothing and baggage, there was very little to be seen. Two or three coats hanging against the partitions had been left behind, but the pockets afforded nothing that yielded any information. There were also a few hats. We opened four satchels and examined the contents, which proved to be nothing but toilet articles, neckwear, handkerchiefs, and so on. We found two Springfield rifles, some ammunition, and some photographic materials. Was n't that about all, Ralph? "

"Yes," said Ralph, "except the fishing-tackle."

"Oh, yes, there were several good poles, lines, fly-books, and trout-baskets. Probably the outlook for trout-fishing was n't very promising when the owners left. On the whole, however, we came to the conclusion that the steamer was not abandoned in great haste. Nearly everything of value for the immediate personal needs of the passengers was missing."

"We noticed another thing," said Ralph, — "there was n't a hairpin or a bonnet or anything that would have belonged to a woman. We decided that the passengers were all men."

"You lads are pretty keen," observed the Captain. "You 'd make first-rate detectives. Why, we 've let a considerable amount of sunshine into this mystery already. It 's plain the Viola was not in regular passenger service. She must have had some special party on board."

Henry nodded assent, and presently proposed that the Captain tell the result of his own investigations.

"Oh, I have n't much of a yarn to spin," said Captain Ayre. "I found about six hundred tons of coal in the bunkers, and the boilers appeared absolutely sound."

"Excellent!" exclaimed Henry. "We could go across the Atlantic."

"The forecastle was as bare as Signal Hill," continued the Captain. "Sailors don't take two or three trunks apiece on a voyage. What little they have they can tie in a bundle and carry off. I looked into the forward hold then, thinking Andy and Phil might not have time. There 's nothing there but lumber and spare rigging. I have n't yet examined the steering gear or the pilot-house thoroughly, but that I 'll do after dinner."

"Can we take her to St. John's then?" asked Phil, eagerly.

"From present appearances, yes."

"How soon shall we start?"

"I don't know. Perhaps to-morrow."

Phil's face grew long at this. He had hoped they would put to sea at once. Ralph and Andy had more patience and were content to take things as they came.

At this juncture Caesar brought in his "deli-c'sies" in the shape of a rice pudding full of raisins, with side dishes of nuts and dates, all of which were received with joyful exclamations by the "crew."

Dinner over, Captain Ayre sent Phil and Ralph ashore with a spyglass, instructing them to climb the cliffs to some commanding spot and watch for intruders by land or sea. They were to give timely warning of such to those on the Viola. Henry and Malcolm, with Andy to help, were detailed to make ready the fires under the boilers, but they were not to light them until further notice. They could call upon Caesar as soon as the dishes were washed and put away, if they needed him.

Having given these directions, Captain Ayre be-took himself to the pilot-house. He gave the big wheel a few experimental turns, and concluded that the chains connecting it with the rudder were in good working order. Then he examined the interior of the little room. A chart, rolled up, and lying upon a cushioned seat, first caught his eye, and he picked it up and spread it out. It proved to be a chart of the coast of Labrador. Next he opened a small white paper which had been inside the roll. This he found was a drawing of much importance. It showed the entire coasts from Long Island Sound to northern Greenland, and indicated, moreover, by a dotted line, the intended course of the Viola. The line began at New York, and made it plain that the voyagers had expected to touch at Sydney on Cape Breton Island, at St. John's in Newfoundland, at Hamilton Inlet in Labrador, and at several settlements in Greenland, even going as far north as Peary's headquarters, beyond Melville Bay. This fully confirmed a suspicion which had been in the Captain's mind that the Viola was a steamer which had put in at St. John's some weeks before in his absence. Upon his return he had been told of the expedition, but the name of the steamer had slipped from his memory. Some misfortune must have befallen the passengers and crew on their way north.

The Captain considered the new information of so much importance that he decided to impart it to Mr. Hollister at once. Not knowing whether that young gentleman was in the engine-room or the stoke-hold, he refrained from ringing the engineer's bell, and started down in person with the map. He had entered and left the pilot-house heretofore by the starboard door, but now he passed out on the port side. As he did so he noticed on the deck near the rail a basket containing a large dark bottle. Though not addicted to bottles in general, the Captain was attracted to this one by curiosity. It was not a place where one would expect to find such an article. He picked it up, and holding it to the light saw that it held a paper.

"Ah, ha!" thought he, "here's some message, or I'm a land-lubber. Clever scheme, too. The paper's in the bottle so that it will float if the steamer founders. The bottle's in the basket so that it won't be broken rolling about. The basket's in a strange place to be the more noticeable, and near the pilot-house so that it could n't be missed. I must read that paper before I'm a minute older."

With this idea he attempted to pull out the cork; but as the cork was in to stay he broke the neck of the bottle. Taking out the paper, he unfolded and eagerly scanned it. As he did so his face brightened. Then he started below in great haste.

Henry, at work with Malcolm and Andy under the boilers, was surprised to see the Captain come down the fire-room ladder at breakneck speed.

"Anything wrong?" he asked in some alarm.

"The mystery is solved!" cried the Captain, waving his papers dramatically as he reached the bottom. "Read this." He handed to Henry the paper from the bottle, and to Malcolm the map,

Andy meantime looking from one to another, more mystified than ever. What Henry read was as follows:

DAVIS STRAIT, July 4.

Steamer Viola with Professor Roth's Arctic expedition is fast in the ice. We have lost our reckoning, but think ship is in latitude about 65 and four miles off Greenland coast. She is likely to be crushed, and we are going ashore over the ice. We have provisions for three weeks. Prompt assistance urgently needed.

WILLIAM BARRETT,

Master S. S. Viola.

3

CHAPTER IV

THE PRIZE CREW AT WORK

RALPH and Phil returned from shore duty when summoned by Caesar's supper-bell, the sound of which came plainly up to their perch on the cliffs. They reported seeing the smoke of a steamer on the southeastern horizon, but no craft had approached the little bay, and no person had appeared on such parts of the island as were visible.

"But what else do you think we saw?" said Phil, as he and Ralph took their seats at the table.

"A seal?" asked Malcolm, at a hazard.

"No."

"A whale?" inquired Andy.

"No. Two big icebergs! We thought at first they were sails, but the glass brought them out quite distinctly. They were far away to the east."

"Oh, they're common enough round here," said the Captain. "I wonder we did n't see any on our run from St. John's. They 'll be drifting past from the north all summer. Some will get stranded and melt near the shore, and some will melt out in the warm water of the Gulf Stream. I 've more startling news than that," and he read aloud the letter which he had found in the bottle.

" What 's the use of going to St. John's, anyway ? " said Phil, with sudden inspiration. " I think we ought to go to Greenland right away and rescue those people. If we don't, they may starve, and then it would be our fault."

Ralph and Andy and Malcolm warmly seconded Phil's bold suggestion, but Henry knit his brows. The possibility of such a thing had already occurred to him, but he saw that the undertaking was too serious to be lightly entered upon.

" Captain," he said at length, " you hear what the lads are saying. Tell me candidly what you think. Is it out of the question or not ? "

" Well, Mr. Hollister," was the reply, " I don't like to say either yes or no too quickly. I must get my bearings. But it 's certainly a case that calls for prompt action of some kind."

" Let 's see," said Henry. " The Viola's people were able to take off provisions for three weeks. That was on the Fourth of July. It 's now the twenty-third. The three weeks will be up day after to-morrow. We can't possibly reach them in two days. But they must have guns and ammunition and fish-hooks. No doubt they will subsist awhile on sea-fowl and fish and seals."

" That's reasonable," said the Captain.

" Now what did you tell me was the distance to the point they mention ? "

" About twelve hundred miles, as I figure it."

" Dat's a mighty long way ter trabble, sho'," declared Caesar, with a decided shake of the head. He had overheard Captain Ayre's estimate as he entered from the galley with a fresh supply of biscuits. " What'll Marse an' Missus Schuyler say ef I lets Phil go? Dat mus' be mos' up ter de Norf Pole."

" Oh, there's no danger, Caesar," remonstrated Phil. " This steamer is lots bigger than our yacht, and you know Father's been to Europe in her."

" Yas, I knows dat, Phil, but dis am differnt. Dere's icebergs an' polar b'ars an' I dunno what all in dis yere Greenland. I heerd a pow'ful lec'sher 'bout it 'long back." The old man went out again with head still shaking.

" It does n't seem possible," remarked Andy, " that the Viola could drift so far in eighteen days."

" She could n't, — that is, not in calm weather,"

said the Captain. "But you remember, no doubt, that we had a long easterly gale early in July, followed by northerly winds. I reckon the ice was broken up soon after the steamer was abandoned. She must have been driven west into the Labrador current in the next few days. Once in that current, she 'd come south at the rate of three to five miles an hour in ordinary weather. It would only take about sixty-seven miles of drift daily on an average to get her here. That 's a little less than three miles an hour."

"I want to ask you this, Captain," said Henry. "Do you consider the Viola safe for Arctic navigation?"

"No. An iron steamer ought not to go into the ice. She 's as brittle as an egg-shell. That was a foolhardy thing for those people to do. I would only take the Viola north in case of direst necessity. The safest way to do it with this small crew would be to hug the Newfoundland and Labrador coasts and so be near shelter in time of bad weather, then watch our chance and strike across Davis Strait when the outlook is good for a few fair days. The ice is probably more scattered or melted by this time, but you never can be sure."

"We could make the Greenland coast in a week,

could n't we, Father?" asked Malcolm, who had been busily figuring with pencil and paper to the partial neglect of his supper.

"Hardly, my lad. There'll surely be fog and the contrary current, and there may be ice and head winds and a breakdown or two in the machinery. Safer to call it two weeks."

"Every moment is precious, then," said Henry. "We must either start for St. John's at once, which would mean plenty of assistance eventually but with the loss of several days, or undertake the rescue ourselves and head the Viola directly north to-night. Am I right, Captain?"

"Quite so, sir."

"If we proceed north," Henry continued, "we shall incur more and greater risks than in taking the Viola down to St. John's, and I don't think we'd be justified unless it's reasonably clear that the lives of the passengers and crew may depend upon it. Do you believe this to be the case, Captain?"

The boys looked anxiously at Captain Ayre. Apparently his answer would tip the scales for or against the most extraordinary adventure that had ever fallen in their way. Caesar, who had come in again, also eyed him intently.

Captain Ayre took plenty of time. At last he said, "If they 've landed on an uninhabited strip of the coast they will need us badly. They may have reached a settlement. Sukkertoppen is in about the latitude mentioned, but we don't absolutely know that they 're there. In view of the uncertainty, I should say that it is our duty to aid them at the earliest possible moment."

"That settles it," said Henry. "However, no member of this party must go against his own will or best judgment."

He cast an inquiring glance over the group, but saw only sparkling eyes and eager looks. Even Caesar offered no objection, for he perceived that the emergency demanded the sacrifice of ordinary precautions, and he trusted to being able to look out for Phil through thick and thin.

Their course having been thus determined and supper over, all repaired to the pilot-house except Caesar, who had the dishes to wash and put away. The sun was sinking in the southwest, behind the hills of Bacalieu. Every trace of mist had vanished, and the suggestion of grayness on the eastern horizon was nothing more than the first faint hint of twilight. Captain Ayre swept the dark blue ocean with his glass, but could see neither sail nor smoke.

Only the two distant icebergs broke the level expanse.

"It has the look of fair weather," said he. "We must take advantage of it and get under way tonight. Mr. Hollister, you will please start the fires. Take Ralph and Andy to help you with the coal. Malcolm, you and Phil turn in and get some sleep. We'll have to call you up about midnight."

Phil would have liked to be on hand at the beginning of the voyage; but seeing Malcolm walk away obediently, and having a great admiration for that young sailor, he too accepted the orders philosophically. Together they picked out a stateroom, agreeing that it would be pleasanter to be room-mates than to bunk apart. They made up the berths with their camping blankets and some of the Viola's sheets, and were soon tucked snugly away, though to Phil, excited by wonderful anticipations, sleep did not come for a long two hours, and he could not resist the temptation to talk to Malcolm.

In the meantime the fires were lighted. Henry and Andy and Ralph, working like beavers, brought coal from the bunkers and threw shovelful after shovelful into the open maws of the furnaces. They had donned the oldest clothes they possessed, and cared no more for the grime and dust than seasoned firemen. But in some respects they were not yet hardened. Their backs began to ache and their hands to blister; and when Captain Ayre and Caesar came down to help them, the three were obliged to leave their work to procure thick gloves. Thus equipped, they went pluckily at it again, and presently acquired the trick of spreading the coal evenly, over the fire wherever there was need. The Captain expressed his satisfaction at their progress, and soon climbed out by the ladder.

The heat in the fireroom at length became so great that the stokers stripped off most of their clothing. Even then the perspiration oozed from every pore. Andy suffered as little inconvenience as any, being accustomed to manual labor on the farm. Henry, too, with the single exception of the blisters, endured the work well. It was Ralph who underwent the hardest experience, for his muscles were as yet untrained. He was therefore relieved after two hours by Caesar, and went in search of the Captain to report for other duty.

He found that mariner on the forward deck, testing the donkey-engine; for steam was now up, and this secondary engine, employed for weighing anchor, hoisting and lowering cargo, and warping the ship into a desired position by a hawser, was an exceedingly useful and necessary part of the equipment.

It took its steam from the boilers of the regular engines. A few trials sufficed to show that it was in good working order.

"Now, Ralph," said the Captain, "tell your brother that I 'm going out in a small boat to take soundings, and that you 're coming with me."

When Ralph returned, the Captain was already in the boat, oars in hand, awaiting him. There was still plenty of daylight for their purpose.

"You sit in the bow there, Ralph, and take it easy," said the Captain. "Your hands are in bad shape, I 'm thinking, eh ? "

"They are rather sore, sir," Ralph admitted. "But I can row with gloves on."

"Well, we 'll see later. Just now I 'm going to let you do the sounding."

They were a few hundred yards out from the Viola when the Captain drew in his oars and produced a coiled line having pieces of cloth tied about it at intervals of a fathom (six feet). On one end of the line was a great cylinder of lead. He showed Ralph how to hold the coil in his left hand, and how to swing the lead a little forward into the water as they rowed, letting four or five fathoms pay out and then coiling it in again. He explained that the Viola would not draw over fourteen feet of water, so if three of the knots went under the surface before the lead touched bottom the depth was safe. Ralph accordingly stood up in the bow, and the Captain resumed his oars. At first the lad bungled, as was natural. The line inclined to tangle or catch on his fingers, and he imagined that he would not know with much certainty whether the lead reached bottom or not.

"If you think it touches," said the Captain, "look on the lower end. There's fresh tallow there, and the sand or mud will stick to it."

Ralph examined the end of the lead several times, but it was always clean. With practice he gained confidence and skill. They took a straight course about half-way between the points of rock at the mouth of the bay. Here the surf was foaming intermittently among the ledges, though the sea was comparatively calm. On they went directly into the open ocean till they were perhaps a quarter of a mile off shore.

"Now," said the Captain, pulling in his oars again, "if your hands will stand it, Ralph, you may row back and I'll sound." They changed places accordingly.

The Captain was able to sound to a much greater depth than Ralph could. Once on the return he brought up sand and seaweed, but in deep water, and it was evident that there was a safe passage for the Viola midway between the capes.

As they came near the steamer the thin line of smoke rising from her funnel became suddenly dense and black, and drifted back over the land in rolling and ever expanding masses.

" That looks like business ! " exclaimed the Captain, delightedly. "Our firemen are doing themselves credit. We'll get out of here before long. But first let's look after the sloop."

" What are you going to do with her ? " asked Ralph.

" Oh, just tuck her away in some sheltered nook and leave her. Everybody hereabout knows her, and I'll put a letter in her cabin to explain matters."

" I've been thinking," remarked Ralph, " that we ought to let our friends at home know our plans somehow. They'll be scared if they don't hear from us."

" True enough, but I've talked it over with your brother, and he thinks it will do if we write from Labrador. The people at home are liable to worry more after they get the letters than before. It will actually spare them some anxiety if we write only at the last moment."

Ralph now helped to tow the Little Auk to a safe anchorage farther inshore. The letter being pencilled and left in a prominent position in the cabin, the two returned to the Viola.

Henry, finding Andy and Caesar able to manage the fires, had come up to try the engines. He was not sure of the strength of the two hawsers, or rather of their fastenings on the shore, and dared not set the machinery in motion except at the slowest speed; but so far as he could judge there was nothing wrong with the engines or with the screw which they turned at the stern.

On learning these facts, Captain Ayre declared himself ready to clear for the North. Ralph was sent out in the small boat to cast off the bow and stern lines from the rocks. The boat was then hoisted to the davits by the donkey-engine, Ralph remaining in it until he could jump out on the Viola's deck. The Captain then went to the pilot-house and Henry to the engine-room, after directing Ralph to haul in and coil the hawsers.

Presently the deep whistle of the Viola startled the sea-fowl on their rocky roosts and reverberated from the hills. There was a ringing of the engine-bells, followed by the slow thud of the machinery. Ralph, as he tugged at the stern line, saw the foam and eddies drift out and away as the steamer made headway, and his heart gave an exulting leap.

They were really off for Greenland, that wonderful region of mysteries. The Viola swung round in an easy circle and passed out to the open sea just as the late dusk was deepening over the land and water.

Malcolm and Phil meanwhile had caught some snatches of sleep. At midnight Henry knocked at their door. They woke with a start. The water was plashing along the steamer's side under the open port-hole, and the steady throb of the engines confirmed the welcome suspicion that the voyage had begun. They hastily dressed and reported to Henry in the engine-room.

"Hello!" said the latter, as they appeared. "You certainly didn't waste much time. There's something to eat in the saloon. Better have a little food first, then go down and relieve Andy and Caesar. You know what to do, Malcolm, and you can teach Phil. They'll show you where they keep their drinking-water. You'll need a good deal of it before you're through. I'll be down occasionally to help you."

The two went off to carry out these instructions, and soon Andy and Caesar came up, hot and tired, and quite ready to take their turn at sleeping. As for Henry and the Captain, there could be no sleep for them so long as the steamer was in motion, and she must move so long as weather permitted.

Phil gave out in the fire-room as Ralph had done; but after an hour's rest, during which Henry took his place, he went back and found that he could stand the work better than at first. Henry continued to make frequent trips back and forth, for the night was clear and the engines needed little attention beyond oiling.

At four o'clock Malcolm and Phil were relieved in turn by Caesar and Andy. All day it was turn and turn about. Each member of the little crew willingly assisted wherever he was needed most, and the Captain held the wheel except at meal-time, when Malcolm took his place. While off duty the boys obtained what sleep they could, and by that means kept themselves comparatively refreshed. Their muscles grew very lame from the unusual exercise of shovelling, but they knew that, as the soreness wore away, their bodies would become toughened to the work.

Captain Ayre declared he had never seen a more beautiful day at sea than that one. The wind was light from the west, the water like a mirror, and the sky a clear, deep blue. It was cool in the shadow of the wheelhouse, — a little too cool, but deliciously warm in the sun. From morning till night there were icebergs in sight, usually several at a time.

Excited and interested as they were, Andy and Ralph and Phil had little time to observe these glistening masses, though Phil took a few snap-shots with his camera at some of the nearer ones. They noticed, however, the great diversity of the icebergs in shape and size. Some were merely small cakes, while others towered two or three hundred feet in air, and must have extended much farther beneath the surface of the sea. One was like a huge castle of purest marble, with turrets and ramparts of medieval architecture rising above the blue water. Another resembled a white cat, half submerged, with head turned back. Another represented a high boot of gray felt. Still others were as flat as a marble table, or conical like a tent. As a rule, wherever the sun shone on it the ice was dazzling white, but in the shadows it was light blue, and under the water-line a delicate green. In some of the ice-walls were blue caves and grottoes into which the ocean swell poured and foamed. What wonder that the boys looked on these wanderers from the Northland with admiration shading strongly into awe!

One of the icebergs changed its plane of equilib-

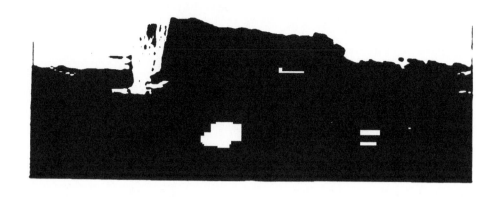

"Icebergs in sight." (*Page* 48.)

rium when the Viola was not far distant. Slowly it rolled over, and then swung back and forth in gradually lessening arcs till it came to rest in its new position. When near the horizon the bergs were more or less altered in appearance by mirage, which sometimes caused simply an abnormal looming, but occasionally painted in the sky an inverted iceberg resting upon the peak of the real one below. These strange apparitions dissolved as the steamer approached, leaving the true iceberg in its proper outlines.

The Viola made good progress until early the following morning, when a heavy fog settled down. Captain Ayre signalled for slow speed and blew the whistle at frequent intervals. When Caesar's bell rang, the engines were stopped entirely, since the crew was unable to furnish a lookout at the bow during breakfast. Malcolm kept the whistle sounding, while his father and Henry at the breakfast-table discussed the question of going forward during fogs. Captain Ayre explained the dangers that threatened, and both men agreed that under ordinary circumstances it would be wise to let the Viola drift until the weather cleared. But as time was valuable and lives might be saved in the present instance, they decided to advance at about half speed, detailing

4

Malcolm to watch at the bow, while Caesar was to take Malcolm's turn in the fire-room. If necessary all cooking was to be dispensed with and salt meat and canned goods were to be relied upon until conditions bettered.

In pursuance of this plan the Viola went forward again at about seven miles an hour as soon as the meal was finished. At eight o'clock, just as Andy and Ralph were handing their shovels over to Phil and Caesar, there came a sudden shock which threw Caesar entirely off his feet. Andy saved himself by catching at the ladder, while Phil and Ralph went over against a bulkhead like two tenpins. "Shipwreck!" was the instant and terrifying thought of all four.

CHAPTER V

THE VIOLA IN COLLISION

IN order to understand what had happened, we must go back to the moment when Captain Ayre returned to the pilot-house after finishing his breakfast. He had found Malcolm keeping a sharp lookout in the intervals between the blasts of the whistle; but so thick was the gray mist about them that the keenest eye could not penetrate it much more than three ship-lengths. The Captain took the whistle-cord and sent his son below for breakfast; but Malcolm was soon back again, munching ham and hardtack on the way so as to save time.

"Now, Malcolm," said his father, "we're going ahead at half speed. You are to stand watch on the bow, and you know the responsibility well enough. Put on an overcoat or a reefer. You'll need it. We're now between Belle Isle and the Labrador coast. It's a bad place. If you see anything ahead, sing out, and be lively about it."

"All right, sir," Malcolm answered, and was off to his post, where he began pacing to and fro across the bow. The cold fog blew over the rail against his face as the Viola moved forward. It collected in fine particles on his reefer and cap. It dropped from the rigging and stood in beads on woodwork and iron. The ominous sound of the whistle seemed to carry but a little distance in that heavy atmosphere. Malcolm, however, gave no heed to anything but his work, and kept his eyes fixed on the indefinite line forward where the dark water blended into the gray.

It was a harder task than one would imagine, — that unwavering concentration of the attention on blank space. Had Malcolm not been accustomed to it 'from previous voyages, his father would not have felt justified in placing the exacting duty upon him now. If his mind wandered even for an instant, that instant's distraction might prove fatal to the ship and crew. Not only must his eyes be riveted upon the utmost line of vision, but the thought also must remain focussed there to the exclusion of everything else.

Before Malcolm had been many minutes on the bow he discovered several small pieces of ice floating some distance to starboard, and promptly shouted to his father. He knew it would not do to overlook even these diminutive fragments, for they might have been broken from an iceberg not far away. He now went close to the rail and strained his eyes forward, for the berg, if there were one, lay quite possibly in the steamer's path. It did not prove to be so, however. After a few seconds the young look-out became conscious, partly by the sense of sight and partly by the sense of hearing, that the object of his search was a little farther to starboard than the small pieces had been. As the steamer swept by he could just see the base of the berg at the water-line, the upper parts being indistinguishable from the mist, and he could hear a faint reflection or echo of the steamer's swash, augmented, no doubt, by the surf around the berg itself. This, then, was a danger past, and he put it at once out of his mind in order that every faculty might be alert for those yet to come.

A half-hour passed without an alarm of any kind. At the end of that time he sighted a few more fragments to starboard not fifty feet from the Viola's course, and before he could turn to give word of them he imagined that the dim line where the mist and water blended forward had grown almost imperceptibly whiter. In the next second he was sure of it, and tearing off his cap he waved it wildly at the pilot-house, shouting " Iceberg ahead! "

He did not wait for another look, but rushed for the upper deck to help his father.

Captain Ayre could not see the berg at all when Malcolm gave the signal, but in a second or two he did, and threw the wheel hard over, then rang for full speed astern. Henry, though fearful lest some part or other might not stand the strain, reversed the engines instantly, and then waited anxiously at his post, unable to see the danger, but made fully aware of it by the sudden and unusual signal. He could not, however, leave the engine-room even for a moment. Everything might depend on his presence and promptness.

In giving the wheel a turn, Captain Ayre had hoped to be able to steer entirely clear of the iceberg. But, as that whiteness at the fog-and-water line grew more distinct and longer and higher, he saw that any attempt to avoid a collision by turning involved the risk of striking a side blow, and that would certainly crush the Viola's iron plates. So he wrenched the wheel back again almost instantly and held the steamer to her former course, pointing her straight for the berg. Malcolm at that moment threw open the door, and, thinking that his father had surely been able to change the direction somewhat, was horrified to see the great mass looming

up squarely over the bow. He would have seized
the wheel, but his father cried quickly, " Steady,
boy, steady! We must strike on the stem. It's
our only chance."

Meanwhile more of the ice-monster had become
visible. What had been but an indistinct line of
white on the water, now loomed up as a snowy wall
as high as the steamer's masts. It was a grand and
awful sight to the two in the pilot-house, but of those
below no one except Henry had so much as a suspicion of the impending catastrophe. True, the
vessel was trembling with the struggles of her screw
as it churned the water into foam, but the four in
the fire-room had been moving about too busily
to notice it. To Malcolm, as he stared helplessly
through the window, it seemed as if some unseen
power thrust the unwilling ship forward, while she
shrank and quivered like a living thing and did her
best to stop. That she could not in that short distance was quickly evident. Malcolm wondered if
the shock would throw him down, and afterward
he remembered stepping back from the window and
bracing his feet to determine that point.

The next instant the ice-wall towered almost over
them. Then the bow rose a little as it touched a
sloping submerged projection. The stem pushed

through the soft snow and melting ice of the berg's exterior to a depth of several feet, — then crash! and a succession of sharp, cracking sounds, and blocks of ice came tumbling upon the bow as the Viola went slowly astern.

Malcolm had been too well prepared for the sudden loss of headway to be thrown down or even much shaken. As for his father, he was still grasping the wheel. In the ice-wall the two saw a deep wedge-shaped scar, its sides streaked with red and black paint. That was all the damage the iceberg had sustained. It remained to determine how the Viola had fared.

" Take the wheel, Malcolm," cried the Captain, " and signal Mr. Hollister to stop. I'll see how bad it is."

With that he hastened down to the forward deck and leaned out over the rail on the port side, expecting to see the water pouring into a large hole. Instead, nothing out of the ordinary appeared. Then he looked over the starboard rail, and at first saw nothing wrong there either. But, chancing to glance higher, he discovered the source of those sharp, cracking sounds. Two of the iron plates nearly up to the deck-level had been bent inward, the seam between them opened wide, and the rivets shattered. The end of the hawse-pipe on that side was crushed, and a part of the rail had been splintered. With a sigh of intense relief the Captain concluded that the whole force of the blow had been received far above the water-line, and the stem had taken the brunt of it as he had intended.

In his father's absence Malcolm called down the tube and acquainted Henry with the situation, and the latter for the first time felt free to leave his post and go on deck. He joined the Captain at the bow, and learned from him the particulars of the accident and the extent of the injury. Both agreed that it would be well to examine the bow from the inside, to be perfectly sure that the ship had sprung no leak. They had just turned to carry out this decision when they caught sight of Caesar tugging at the canvas covering of one of the boats amidships.

"What can he be up to?" queried Henry.

Not being able to advance any theory, the Captain shouted, "Hi, there, Caesar! what's the matter with that canvas?"

"I'se got dis boat mos' ready, Marse Cap'n," yelled Caesar, excitedly, in reply. "Ef yo''ll jes' come hyah an' fin' de oars, I'll run an' git Phil an' de rest. Is we sinkin' fast?"

"Oh, no, Caesar," replied the Captain, with diffi-

culty suppressing a smile; "we 're all right, I reck'n."
Then to Henry he added, "Suppose you look after
Caesar and the boys, Mr. Hollister, while I go through
the forward hold alone."

They parted accordingly, and Henry walked aft
along the deck. On approaching Caesar, he was
surprised to find that not only had the man removed
the canvas, but in accomplishing it he had cut all the
small cords which held the covering in place at the
edges.

"Why, Caesar!" exclaimed Henry, "you 've
done a lot of mischief here. Why did n't you wait
for orders?"

"Ter tell de troof, Marse Henry," answered the
cook, with evident remorse, "dar was n't no one
givin' no orders, an' I reckoned dar orter be one
boat dat I could put young Phil into. I 'se pow'ful
sorry I cut de ropes, but I 'll repa'r 'em, Marse
Henry. Sho 's yo' bawn, I will."

"All right, Caesar. Never mind. Don't feel
bad about it. I know you did only what you thought
was necessary, — and it might have been too. Where
are the boys?"

"Dey 's in de fire-room, — Phil an' Ralph an'
Andy."

"You don't mean they stayed down there through

all this?" Henry looked as if he would have liked to believe it, however, incredulous though he was.

"Not 'zac'ly," Caesar answered. "I 'low dey all come up dat ladder after dat smash an' tek a squint for'ard, but dey all look back like dey was leavin' de post ob duty. Den Andy, he say he gwine down an' look after de fires, an' de rest could go see what's de matter. Ralph and Phil, dey say dey go down too, an' I mus' fin' out 'bout de ship an' let dem know. Den I goes up for'ard an' sees dat iceberg, an' I done put fo' de boat hot-foot. Dat's all I know 'bout it."

"We'd better go now and relieve their anxiety," said Henry, and together they hastened down to the fire-room, where they found the three lads at work. Very glad indeed were the three to see Henry and Caesar, and to learn that the Viola was safe. Henry complimented them heartily on their excellent conduct during a most trying experience, but they insisted that Caesar deserved the most commendation.

"Why, he wanted to take care of the fires all alone," said Ralph, enthusiastically. "He begged us to go and save ourselves. It was all we could do to send him away from the fire-room."

"Ah!" exclaimed Henry, thoughtfully, and he looked at the black man with added comprehension

and admiration. " Well, all I can say is that we 've
a mighty good crew, even if it is a small one."

Meanwhile Captain Ayre had completed his investigation forward, and came to the top of the ladder
to call for Henry, who went up at once. At Henry's
suggestion, the three lads were also allowed to come
on deck and refresh themselves a little, Caesar volun-
teering to keep the fires. This was a comparatively
simple matter while the steamer was at rest and the
furnace doors could be left open to check the draft.

The five repaired to the wheelhouse, where Malcolm
was on guard. Captain Ayre reported that all was
well below decks. He asked Henry's opinion as to
what should be done, stating that, as near as he
could judge by the log, the steamer was about five
miles northwest of Belle Isle and not far from the
southeast shores of Labrador. After a conference
the two decided that an effort should be made to
repair the two bow plates and the end of the hawse-
pipe before advancing farther north. There might
be a blacksmith at Cape Charles Harbor, the nearest
fishing village of Labrador, and in any event that
port offered temporary shelter until their further
course could be determined.

By this time the fog began to lift and disperse,
disclosing their old enemy, the iceberg, not far away,

with the dent plainly visible in its side. Soon they discovered that the sea to the north was almost covered with bergs.

" Look there!" cried Captain Ayre. "We couldn't have picked a straight course anywhere in that direction without striking one or another of those fellows," — which was true, and, on the whole, they might have fared much worse.

From Malcolm the three young stokers learned the particulars of the accident, and the four compared notes with much interest while the Captain and Henry were talking together. Presently Malcolm and Phil were sent to relieve Caesar, it being properly their turn in the fire-room. They were to inform Caesar that, as the fog had cleared, he could return to the galley and prepare a good dinner.

The northern end of Belle Isle was in sight eastward as the boys started below. Andy and Ralph remained with the Captain in the pilot-house, while Henry went back to the engines. The Viola was soon under way again, and approached the Labrador coast to the west. A little later there were charming views of this mainland. Before noon the Viola entered Cape Charles Harbor, passing for half a mile or more through a narrow channel bordered by rocky hills of smooth, glaciated contour, patched with green. Low-lying reefs were numerous, and in among them were dories whose occupants were catching codfish. They stared at the Viola in surprise, for steamers were rare in those parts.

The harbor appeared to extend inland several miles, but presently, where it first widened, the signal was given to stop. All hands were now called to the forward deck, and under Henry's supervision the port anchor was raised by the donkey-engine from its resting-place, swung out from the bow, and let go into the water, the huge chain paying out with a great rumbling until the bottom was reached. The voyagers found themselves in plain view of a little fishing hamlet that nestled about a cove to the south not far from their anchorage.

CHAPTER VI

CAPE CHARLES HARBOR, LABRADOR

AFTER dinner Malcolm, Andy, Ralph, and Phil were detailed to row over to the settlement and make inquiries for an ironworker. Their shore leave was to be three hours long, and in their absence the Captain and Henry planned to get the sleep of which they stood in great need. Caesar was to bank the fires with ashes so that they would need little attention, and stand watch over the ship in general.

The boys, after a last attempt to get the coal-dust out of their hair and eyes, lowered one of the green dories, several of which were nested on the Viola's deck in addition to the regular boats, and were soon pulling away toward the cove. Ralph took with him the tin case in which he had collected botanical specimens in Newfoundland, and Phil carried his camera. They landed on the rocky shore near the village, where it was agreed that Malcolm and Andy should obtain what information could be had in the village, leaving Ralph and Phil free to search as widely as they liked for plants and pictures.

Phil desired first to scale the bleak hills across the cove, whence, he thought, fine views could be enjoyed. This was agreeable to Ralph, since those same hills would doubtless furnish good specimens of Arctic vegetation. The two therefore entered the dory again and rowed across the short space of calm water.

The climbing on the far side was exceedingly rough. Here and there was a smooth bit of green grass, but for the most part the way was over jagged, broken rocks and up steep slopes and cliffs. Phil's camera was of the old tripod type, and somewhat unwieldy. He had beside to carry a supply of heavy plates eight inches long by five wide. Many times he regretted that he had not brought a camera of the light, film-carrying variety. But with Ralph's help he struggled up the heights as best he could.

From an elevation of several hundred feet the outlook was both extensive and beautiful. The diminutive village, with its dozen straggling dwellings, its wharves and fish-houses, nearly surrounded the bay below, where a number of stout little sloops and schooners, doubtless built by their owners, lay at

A fishing village in Labrador.   (*Page* 64.)

anchor. Out in the wider bay floated the Viola. Beyond, to the west and north, were hills that showed old snowbanks, bays into which an iceberg or two had drifted, and rocky islands of all sizes.

While Ralph and Phil looked off upon this bleak region, there came clear and sweet to their ears from the village the melody of a hymn which both boys had learned at school. How strange and beautiful to hear it again so far from home, — in fact, right at the verge of Arctic wastes, and sweet as only a child's voice could make it.

The two soon scrambled down again, recrossed the cove, and then climbed the high hills behind the village. Ralph discovered various kinds of grasses and mosses, dwarf spruce, white violets, ferns, heather, and a few little pink and yellow flowers, some of which were blossoming close to a melting snowbank of the previous winter. Phil noticed and photographed a curious formation of bent strata in the rock. The remainder of their time was spent in the village, where they were joined by Malcolm and Andy.

"There is n't a blacksmith in the place," said Malcolm, as they met. "The people we saw don't think there's one anywhere along this coast. Iron is very scarce, and they don't use horses here at all,

so there's no need for an ironworker. I don't kno
how we're ever going to repair the Viola."

" The men are all out fishing," said Andy. " Th
is their busy season. Only the women and childre
are in the village at this time of day. I guess we'
have to make the repairs ourselves."

The two older lads had asked a great many que
tions during their ramble through the settlemen
and they now took Ralph and Phil about and ex
plained many things of interest.

The village was like a hundred others scattere
along those coasts, — in summer the scene of bus
life, in winter deserted by the transient Newfounc
land fishermen, and desolate in its garb of ice an
snow. Even its few permanent families remove
in the autumn to winter dwellings in the shelter o
the spruce and juniper forests inland. In fact, fev
of the coast settlements are inhabited in the wintei
The people are then completely cut off from the res
of the world, but in summer a mail steamer make
fortnightly visits, and trading vessels call for cargoe
of fish.

Of the dozen dwellings at Cape Charles, a fev
were painted or whitewashed, but the majority wen
as gray as the rocks around them. In a conspicuou
position on a ridge at the head of the cove stood ar

edifice of the Church of England. It was about the size and shape of the smallest summer cottages at a New England shore resort, but the wonder was, not that it was little, but that so sparsely settled a colony could build it at all. The Labrador people are simple, true-hearted, God-fearing folk, and they have not outgrown the Church as so many in more favored climes seem to have done.

A flagstaff near the building served for both spire and bell, the display of the flag indicating that some stray preacher was at hand to hold a service. There had been but three services during the summer preceding. Looking through the windows, the boys found that the seats were rude wooden benches without backs. The communion cups and plates were in a little cupboard behind the platform, and much resembled a set of doll's dishes.

Down on the wharves, lightly but strongly built of timbers hewn in the forests of the interior, stood the fish-houses, where the cod — always called by the general term " fish " — were cleaned, salted, and temporarily stored. Curious anchors known as killicks, constructed of wood and weighted by stones in the absence of iron, lay about the wharves. On the roofs of the buildings, or on frames made for the purpose, were stretched the skins of seals, which, being of a kind whose fur is worthless, were saved for the leather. Nets were drying on convenient poles, while against the sides of the buildings stood great casks full of cod livers and oil.

A few of the dwellings were flanked by little gardens where rhubarb and cabbages struggled for existence. There was no street, nor fence, nor boundary line, so far as our young friends could discover. Each man built his house wherever he could find a flat space, and if that were not obtainable the house rested partly on posts. There were a few lonesome-looking hens, a goat or two, and a great many dogs, the latter being of various colors and showing characteristics of both the New-foundland and the Eskimo breeds. Their enforced summer idleness had led them to fight a good deal among themselves, and every dog was abundantly scarred and scratched. Ralph and Phil feared at first that they might prove hostile, but they did not so much as growl, and Malcolm declared that they were not dangerous unless ill-fed.

" I 've heard a story," said he, " about the dogs of Battle Harbor, which is a settlement a few miles north of here. Some years ago the captain of a fishing schooner stopped to pet the dogs as he was walking through the place. They happened to be hungry at the time, and followed him, and began to jump upon him. Finding that what he had taken for a frolic was becoming a serious attack, he defended himself to the best of his ability and shouted for help. The shipmates who responded came too late. They found their captain dead, and in revenge they killed all the dogs in the village. The fishermen were obliged to send for a new supply of puppies, since they relied upon dogs to haul wood and draw sledges in winter."

" I don't believe I 'll stop to pet these fellows," said Phil. " They all look rather wolfish."

The three hours were now nearly spent. The boys had met very few of the fisher-folk, but Malcolm said that a little later in the day this quietness would give way to bustle and activity. His companions hoped that they might then be on hand, but it was now time to return to the ship.

At the supper table the situation was discussed thoroughly. Henry thought it might be possible to cut an iron plate out of the side of a hatchway and bolt it over the open seam on the bow, but this would be a long and tedious job with the few tools at their disposal. Beside, it would close the shattered hawse-pipe entirely. Captain Ayre was inclined to the opinion that further use of the starboard anchor would have to be dispensed with anyway. He thought the crack could be stopped with a mattress and boarded up on the inside so as to be water-tight in case of heavy seas. This would not take long, and would probably serve until the regular crew of the Viola could be reached and put to work on the plates. Henry agreed with this view of the matter, and it was decided to begin the repairs next morning.

After supper the boys were again given their freedom. When the four reached the village, the dories, deep-laden with cod, were arriving. Each bronzed fisherman, picturesque in his rough coat and sou'wester, tossed his fish upon a wharf, whence they were conveyed into the rude buildings at the rear. Just as the long twilight came on, the chill, slimy work of splitting and cleaning began.

All the men, women, and young people were in the fish-houses now, and all except the youngest had a part in the work. By the yellow glare of lanterns the fish were thrown upon the tables and split, the heads and refuse portions removed, the backbone cut out, and the edible remainder tossed into a huge tub of water, thence to be pitchforked into long rows that are plentifully sprinkled with salt as they rise higher and higher. Each worker has one thing to do, and does it deftly and well. They work long into the evening, until the whole day's catch is disposed of.

The boys wondered that people were willing to come from pleasanter lands to this drudgery in a cold and desolate region, where, though the songs of children and the twitter of birds are sometimes heard, there is yet lacking so much that makes life sweet and endurable. But when they expressed such feelings to a venerable, white-bearded fisherman who stood, pitchfork in hand, ready to pile and salt the fish, he answered with a smile, "Yes, I s'pose it's dirty work, my lads, but it makes clean money."

The fisher-folk showed no little interest in the novel undertaking in which the boys were engaged. They listened eagerly to the story of the Viola and the plans of the rescuers, and expressed their wonder at what the little crew had already accomplished. Malcolm invited them all to visit the ship on the following day, and they in turn urged the boys to make themselves at home in any of the humble dwellings of Cape Charles.

The four were too sleepy to remain long ashore. After watching the workers for an hour or so they rowed back to the ship and turned in for a good night's rest. The fires needed little attention, banked as they were, and morning found the prize crew refreshed and ready for business.

The first matter requiring their attention was the open seam in the bow. Repairs were begun by Henry and Andy. Parts of an old mattress were stuffed tightly into the break, which was then covered outside and inside with a framework of boards stout enough to resist any but the most exceptional storm-waves. This gave to the bow a patched appearance, but the application of some black paint from the ship's stores overcame the unsightliness to a considerable extent.

Ralph and Phil, to their great delight, were commissioned to go in search of trout. They set off over the hills with poles and lines and flies, and as the result of whipping a number of lakelets they brought back good strings. These trout were six or eight inches long and much darker than the brook trout of New England. Caesar took charge of them, promising to serve them in fine style later on.

Captain Ayre and Malcolm busied themselves in replenishing the tanks of the Viola, which were nearly empty. This was a slow and tedious process, since the water had to be brought in casks from a brook near the settlement, and many trips were necessary. The work was not finished at noon, and it was clear that even with help from Henry and Andy, who had completed the repairs, the Viola could not get away that day.

"Perhaps it's just as well," remarked the Captain, consolingly, at dinner. "I don't like the looks of the weather. The barometer's falling, and we're likely to get wind and rain and maybe more fog."

"It'll be rather rough on the Viola's people if we're delayed," observed Malcolm. "The three weeks ended yesterday, and they're probably on short rations by this time."

"Possibly," said Henry, "but I don't think they'll suffer just yet if they have firearms and ammunition. We can't be sure that they reached the coast safely. That's the thing that troubles me most. It's conceivable that the ice drifted offshore before they could land, or they might have been unable to save all the supplies which they took out of the ship. We must lose no time in finding them, but of course we can't put to sea in bad weather."

"Isn't the ship seaworthy now?" asked Andy, who had taken a good measure of pride in his share of the repairs.

"Yes," answered the Captain. "She'll do very well, even in a gale, so far as the bow is concerned, but we haven't crew enough to handle her. You

lads might all be sick together, and then we could n't
depend on you, and who 'd do the stoking ? "

"Oh, now, Captain!" said Phil. "That's too
bad. Why, I 've been on the ocean in awfully rough
weather, and I never was sick a bit."

"I guess it would make a difference whether you
were on deck or down in the fire-room," suggested
Ralph, who had already felt some nausea while in
that hot and stuffy place.

"That's the point, my boy," said the Captain.
"I should n't be at all surprised if I were sick
myself in the fire-room. In that condition and with
a cross-sea running I would n't undertake to find
the furnace door with a shovelful of coal more than
once in three or four tries. You 've no idea how
hard it is. You 'd be lucky if you did n't pitch
into the furnace yourself. Fact is, we 've managed
to knock off about a quarter of the distance we 've
got to go, but only by reason of favoring circumstances, and we 'll start again in fair weather or
not at all."

While Caesar cleared away the remains of the
meal, the six went on deck to observe the weather
signs. The sky was overcast with a dull gray
blanket of mist. An east wind was rising and send-
ing choppy little waves dancing in from the harbor's

entrance, past which several icebergs could be seen moving southward. The air felt raw and damp.

Despite the unfavorable outlook, it was decided that Malcolm and Andy and Ralph and Phil should complete the filling of the tanks, so that all might be in readiness for departure. In the meantime the Captain and Henry would write letters to the friends at home explaining the change of plans, for the south-bound mail steamer would soon be due.

As he turned toward the companionway, Captain Ayre happened to glance in the direction of the head of the harbor.

" Hello! " said he. " Who's coming yonder? "

The others looked also, and saw that a heavy rowboat was slowly approaching against the wind. There appeared to be two persons in the boat, — a man and a woman.

" Perhaps they're some of the Cape Charles people," conjectured Malcolm. " I gave them a general invitation yesterday."

" But they're not coming from the settlement," said Henry.

" They might be from Battle Harbor," ventured the Captain. " There's a hospital there, — Dr. Grenfell's. Perhaps they've run out of some kind of medicine and think we 've a doctor aboard. We 'll soon see, anyhow."

⸱ As the boat came alongside, Malcolm ran down the port ladder and made fast a line which was thrown to him by the oarsman. The latter then helped his companion up to the deck. They were young people, not over twenty-five, and both seemed quite bashful as they saw with what interest they were observed by the little party on the steamer. But the man soon plucked up courage.

"Bound north, sir?" he asked, addressing the Captain.

"To Greenland," was the reply.

"Going up for Peary, I s'pose, sir?"

"No, not so far as that."

"Large party?"

"No. Rather small."

"I — I s'pose you 've got a minister aboard?"

"Ah!" exclaimed the worthy Captain, his face broadening into a smile, "I see. You want to get married."

"That 's it, sir."

The young fisherman looked relieved at the display of acumen on the Captain's part, and the intended bride blushed her rosiest, while a smile went round the group.

"We've waited a long time — Mary an' me," the man continued, "an' we hoped your minister could splice us. I can't do very handsome by him, but might he take a couple of salmon?"

"By way of a fee, eh? Yes, I reck'n he would, but I'm sorry to have to tell you there's no sky-pilot aboard the Viola."

The faces of the two fell decidedly at this bad news. They would have to wait weary weeks more — perhaps months. They conferred somewhat apart from the others.

"We'd like to trade the salmon," said the young man, thriftily, after some moments. "Might you have some potatoes?"

"We have," replied the Captain. "Mr. Hollister here is the man to strike the bargain."

"With the greatest pleasure," said Henry. "Bring up your salmon."

The young man returned to his boat and soon appeared with two magnificent specimens.

"What are they worth?" asked Henry.

"Oh, they'll fetch about sixty cents apiece hereabout, sir."

"How many potatoes do you want for them?"

"I'd be glad to get half a bushel. They're scarce and high in these parts."

Henry reflected. There still remained a bushel in the camping supplies, and there were a good many bags among the Viola's stores.

"I'll give you a bushel, and welcome," said he, presently.

Thus the trade was completed to the satisfaction of both parties, and the lovers re-embarked for the long pull homeward.

That afternoon a number of the villagers visited the steamer. Some came in their own boats, and some, especially the children, were conveyed by the four lads on their trips with the water-casks. It was interesting to see with what wonder these strangers looked about them. Our friends learned with surprise that many of the little folk, and even a few of their elders, had never been far enough from Cape Charles to see a horse, or a sheep, or a pig, to say nothing of fine buildings, railroad trains, carriages, and a thousand and one things which children farther south think quite commonplace. The dreary coast of Labrador, with its rocks and bays, its fish and fogs and icebergs, was the only world they knew except by hearsay.

Phil and Malcolm in one boat, and Andy and Ralph with a young Cape Charles boy in another, were setting out to the ship on one of their trips from the village, when a strange series of clanging, metallic sounds came to their ears from a point behind the high hill eastward, and presently ceased.

"What was that?" cried Andy. "Talk about a blacksmith! I should think they had a whole iron foundry somewhere over there."

Since they were quite sure there was only a rockbound and almost uninhabited coast in that direction, neither Phil nor Ralph nor even Malcolm could offer a plausible explanation; but the boy could.

"It's an iceberg breaking up," said he. "We hear them sometimes, and last summer I saw one. The water was all white foam around it when it tumbled apart, and big waves came in on the shore. Oh, it was fine to see, I can tell you!"

"But it sounded just like dropping steel rails one against another," said Ralph. "I don't see how ice could make that kind of a noise."

"It reminded me a little of the sound of weather cracks on a frozen pond or river," said Malcolm. "There's apt to be a metallic ring to such a sound. The boy is undoubtedly right."

That evening the threatened storm arrived, with drizzling rain and a chill sea-wind. But the voyagers, safe in their harbor, had another night of comparatively undisturbed repose. They hoped, when morning came, to find signs of clearing, and in fact the rain had ceased when they turned out on deck, but the east wind still blew too savagely to permit their departure, and — what was more serious — during the night an iceberg of no mean dimensions had drifted into the narrow entrance and grounded squarely across the deepest part. The little group stared at this white visitor with dismay.

"We're blockaded, sure enough!" cried the exasperated Captain. "Mainland to starboard, islands and reefs to port and astern, and a big berg in the channel. Looks encouraging, does n't it?"

"She may go out when the tide turns," said Henry as hopefully as he could, but he had to admit also that the berg might stay a fortnight. The four lads expressed their impatience in unmistakable terms. It was Caesar who accepted the situation most philosophically.

"Dis hyah am a bery respec'able harbor," he declared, "an' a pow'ful sight mo' safer dan de open sea. I ain' findin' no fault."

But Caesar, as we have seen, was no coward. He was thinking only of Phil.

CHAPTER VII

ADRIFT ON AN ICEBERG

THE turn of the tide had no appreciable effect on the iceberg. It was still in the channel at noon, and it was there late at night. The seven on the Viola earnestly hoped that the way would be clear by the time they could venture forth, and they maintained this optimistic frame of mind by keeping busy all day. Caesar repaired the lashings of the canvas coverings which he had cut in the excitement of the collision. The others wrote letters, washed down the decks, and tended the fires.

The boys had heard of good hunting in the forest about nine miles back from the coast, where deer, bears, lynxes, porcupines, grouse, and ptarmigans abounded, and they might have tried their luck had it not seemed inadvisable to go so far from the ship. Instead they went fishing for cod on a near-by shoal that evening. Hardly had they located the fishing ground and come to anchor when the fish took the bait. The cod could be hauled to the surface with scarcely a protest, but there was some sport in feeling the weight of such big fellows on the lines. Between them they caught forty-five. Poor Phil had but one to his credit, as he lost hooks and sinker at the very outset, and then got his line so tangled that it took an hour to straighten it out. By that time the fish had ceased biting.

Another morning found conditions very little changed. The iceberg appeared to have become a fixture in the landscape. The east wind continued strong, and through the gray blanket of the sky the dampness sifted as a coarse mist, softening the outlines of all distant things.

Andy and Ralph and Phil could not endure the thought of remaining cooped up on the steamer. The oilskin suits would protect them from the weather, and both harbor and coast seemed to invite them forth. So, taking Malcolm into their confidence, they held an animated discussion on the subject of an outing. Phil was eager to make photographs of the iceberg at close range. His enthusiasm kindled Andy's. There were several cameras with their outfits on the steamer, and Phil agreed to show Andy how to use one. First, however, they consulted Henry as to the propriety of taking it. Henry decided in the affirmative, saying that the owner could doubtless be reimbursed for the use of his materials later, and would not be likely to grudge his rescuers a favor. Ralph was in hopes of discovering some new plants or flowers, and he signified his intention of taking a shot-gun in case they should see any ducks. Malcolm, for his part, preferred a rifle, declaring that he would like to shoot at a mark if nothing else offered.

It was agreed, with Captain Ayre's permission, to take one of the lifeboats, and to carry food for the midday meal, for there was no knowing how far they might wander by dinner time. As to their route, the Captain restricted them to such portions of the harbor and shores as were in sight of the iceberg, for, if the blockade should be raised, the Viola would go to sea at once, weather permitting. At Henry's suggestion they undertook to visit the post-office on their way and mail the home letters. Food, guns, cameras, and letters being collected, the stanch boat with her crew of four drew away from the big hull of the steamer and headed for the entrance, the Captain and Henry and Caesar leaning over the rail to see them off.

The little dwelling occupied by the postmaster was situated on the seaward side of the promontory which enclosed the cove, and well out toward the stranded iceberg. The boat soon arrived at the land-ing-place, and the boys approached the house by a well-worn path. The building was of wood, rude and unpainted. Ralph noted with interest that bril-liant mosses and little wild-flowers were growing on its roof, seeming to cling there for the warmth that might filter through from the stove within. The postmaster, a Newfoundlander, made this his summer home. Fortunately he was in, and the lads received a cordial welcome.

The room into which they entered contained rough benches, an old stove, a sideboard with a few dishes, a bed, and a chest. It was evident that official duties did not divert much of the postmaster's time from the fishing. An old hat was entirely adequate as a mail-bag, and it was empty until the letters from the Viola imparted a somewhat more prosperous air to it. The hat and the letters were carefully locked up in the chest. No stamps were to be had, but the postmaster accepted the postage money and promised to see that all the letters were stamped when the mail steamer came in. He could not say with certainty when that would be.

From the post-office there was a magnificent view seaward. Not less than a hundred icebergs were in sight, but nearly all were too distant to show well in a picture. The berg in the channel, which was now the objective point, lay perhaps half a mile beyond the post-office, and Phil and Andy, in great haste to be off, led the way back to the boat.

The best spot for picture-taking was the rocky shore on the south side of the entrance. From this shore the berg was but a few rods distant. No rain was now falling, and, though the sky remained overcast, the conditions were not wholly unfavorable to Phil's art. The boy was interested to see that the near end of the big mass of ice presented an excellent profile of the Sphinx, and he placed his camera in the best position for recording this natural piece of sculpture. Andy watched him carefully, and then with some help succeeded in setting up the instrument he had borrowed. They made a number of what promised to be excellent pictures. Malcolm and Ralph were then in favor of rowing or walking along the coast in search of bird or beast, for as yet they had not fired a shot, but Phil had been seized by a bold spirit of adventure.

" Fellows," he proposed, " let's see first if we can climb upon the iceberg. It's the best chance we'll ever have, and perhaps we can take a picture or two right there."

The novelty of this idea appealed strongly to

Ralph and Andy. Malcolm was more experienced, and had misgivings. He had heard of ships destroyed by the collapse of icebergs, and he reminded his companions of the one which had gone to pieces off this very coast a few days before. It was certainly unsafe to be very near such a monster.

"But," said Phil, "if we are on it for only fifteen minutes or so, there surely isn't much chance of its breaking up during that time. Why, just think how long it has been here already!"

"What would Caesar say?" ventured Malcolm, mischievously.

"Caesar's all right, but he isn't here," said Phil, too much in earnest to make light of Malcolm's question.

"What would the Captain or Henry say?" put in Andy.

"They aren't here either," replied Phil.

Malcolm laughed. "That's rather a rebellious mood you're in, youngster," he observed. "Anybody would think you didn't care what they would say."

"Oh, I didn't mean that," said Phil, quickly. "But I don't see why we can't decide this for ourselves."

Ralph, who heretofore had only listened, now

suggested that they row around the berg to see if it looked threatening. This plan was accepted by the others as a satisfactory compromise, and the four re-embarked with the cameras.

The length of the berg might have been four hundred feet, its width two hundred, and its height fifty. The loftiest and most solid portions seemed to be the northern and southern ends, the centre being about fifteen feet lower. Near the top of the southern knob, which formed the head of the Sphinx, the ice was honeycombed into little caves. Along the middle of the berg, as the boat approached it, a low platform or ledge was observed which in places appeared quite level and accessible.

Passing between the southern end and the rocks, the youthful explorers rowed out in the teeth of the wind to examine the seaward side. There the waves were foaming and splashing into great blue and white caves or lapping at solid white walls, while under the water-line, as they had before observed, the ice seemed tinted with emerald. The inspection of this part of the berg was not very reassuring. The disintegrating process was evidently well begun. So many arches and pinnacles and caves showed that the sea was undermining and the wind gnawing away the great structure. A little out from the

base of the southern end stood a mushroom-shaped
pedestal which, above water, had melted away from
the main mass, but was still joined to it beneath.

" I don't like the looks of things," declared Malcolm, as they turned to row back. " This is not half
so solid as the one we struck. That was a big square
block of a berg, but this is full of cracks and holes."

" Well," said Phil, " let's go on it, anyhow, and
take our pictures and get off again. I 'll risk it."

Ralph had been scrutinizing the ice with the eye
of a scientist.

" If we should stand on that level platform on
the harbor side," said he, " there would be no overhanging parts to fall on us, and I should think that
at the first sign of trouble we could slip safely off
into the boat."

" I 'm not so sure," said Malcolm. " We might
be thrown into the water and crushed between heavy
pieces or drowned. I 'd soon enough chance it
myself, but if anything happened to you fellows,
Father and Mr. Hollister would blame me. Father
would say I ought to have known enough about icebergs to keep away from them. What do you think,
'Andy ? "

" Why, I hardly know what to think," was the
answer. " It 's easy to see what might happen, and

yet I suppose the chances are in our favor if we don't stay long. I hardly think we ought all to go on the berg at once. If two of us went, the other two could take the boat to a safe distance so that it would n't be swamped by a break-up. Otherwise we might lose our only means of rescue."

This idea, after debate, was decided to be a good one. It was then determined that Phil and Andy should be first to scale the side of the berg, while Malcolm and Ralph in the boat should be ready to render instant assistance. Malcolm consented to the whole undertaking only when positively assured that each one would assume entire responsibility for himself.

By this time the force of the wind had blown the boat some distance past the berg and into the entrance, and it was only with good strong pulling at the oars that she was rounded to and brought up in the lee of the ice toward the ledge. She was within a hundred feet of it when, without warning, a chunk of the rim weighing five or six tons broke off, splashed into the water, and floated away. Ralph, who was holding the tiller-ropes, saw it fall. The others heard the sound and turned in time to realize the cause.

With one consent Malcolm and Andy and Phil

stopped rowing and gazed at the place of cleavage. There was absolutely nothing to show that the ice which had fallen had not been perfectly sound and hard. All along the ledge, except that one spot, still remained a projecting rim about three feet above the water. Underneath it the ice had been melted by the waves and sloped backward. Above this rim the surface of the ledge was rounding and as slippery as glare ice could make it. The top of the platform where level footing could be had was about six feet above the water and several feet back from the rim. It was not going to be easy or even safe to climb upon the level place, but the warning fall of ice came too late to deter the boys. No doubt it was foolhardy, but they had made up their minds to stand upon that berg, and after a few seconds they resumed their rowing.

Ralph guided the boat to a little cleft twenty feet to the right of the spot where the break had occurred. Andy drew in his oars, seized the boat-hook, and began prodding the ice here and there. He found it hard and smooth.

"You'll have to jab the hook in as high up as you can," said Malcolm, "and pull yourself up by that."

Andy acted on this suggestion. Having fastened

" After a few seconds they resumed their rowing."   (*Page* 90.)

the hook securely, he gave a jump that sent the boat
bounding back and threatened to dislodge the iron
point on which he depended. For a moment it was
an even question whether he would gain the ledge
or slip back into the water. The next instant he
had recovered his balance and taken a fresh hold
with the hook farther up, which brought him to
the top of the slope. In the meantime Malcolm
pulled the boat close in again in spite of wind and
waves, which, even on the lee side of the berg, drove
the craft with considerable force.

When the cameras had been passed up, it was
Phil's turn to jump. His landing was accomplished
in a similar manner, except that in his eagerness
to make sure of a footing he sprang rather too
far, and was obliged to put on brakes at the top
or he would have gone clear over into a pond
which he was surprised to see in a deep hollow
beyond.

" A little more, Andy," he cried, as he scrambled
to his feet, " and you would have had to fish me
out of that hole. Why did n't you give me a
warning ? "

" I did n't suppose you were coming like a can-
non-ball," answered Andy. " Anyhow, you 're safe
enough now so long as you don't go too near the

edge. There's not any too much standing-room here."

In fact there was hardly more than space enough to set up the tripods, and in stepping around them the boys had to keep the boat-hook handy against a slip. The tripods were fortunately provided with iron spikes which gave them a good grip. As quickly as possible the cameras were made ready and pointed so as to include the pond and the southern end of the berg. Phil now made the provoking discovery that he had lost the cap from his lens. Probably it was on the rocks where he had taken his last picture. He shouted to Malcolm and Phil, who were rowing away, and they promptly returned. On learning what was wanted Malcolm offered to join Andy on the berg while Phil and Ralph rowed to the shore and searched for the cap. The two exchanged places with some difficulty, and again the boat drew away, while Andy proceeded with his picture-taking.

About ten minutes had elapsed after the departure of their younger companions when both Malcolm and Andy felt a very distinct vibration pass through the ice under their feet, accompanied by a dull crunching sound. Andy cast a startled glance of inquiry at Malcolm. The latter had instantly recognized the cause of the phenomenon.

" She 's grinding against the bottom," he declared. " Listen! There it is again."

" Will she break up, do you think ? " asked Andy, anxiously.

" Can't tell. If she gets in motion and then hits a rock she 'd probably go all to smash. She won't stand much jarring, that 's certain. We 'd better call for the boat."

They could see Ralph and Phil in the distance walking about on the weather-worn rocks with their heads bent down, and they shouted at the top of their lungs, not doubting that their voices would easily carry with the wind. Yet the searchers continued their work without even looking up.

" Must be pretty thoroughly absorbed," said Andy.

" Oh, they 'd look if they heard," Malcolm declared. " I believe the wind is in their ears. Why did n't I keep that gun by me ? Let 's yell together."

They tried it, but with no better success. And now arose a new complication. Malcolm happened to glance past the end of the berg at the nearest point of the shore and discovered that the iceberg was moving out to sea. He communicated this fact excitedly to Andy, and both redoubled their efforts to attract the attention of the two on the rocks. Once Ralph looked up, but it was only for an instant, and doubtless to his eyes the iceberg appeared as stationary as ever. Had it been more than a momentary glance, he could not have failed to see that Andy and Malcolm were waving their arms. As it was, he noticed nothing unusual, and their search presently took the two entirely out of sight of the berg behind some boulders.

Phil at length espied the missing article in a crevice whither it had rolled or been blown, and the two then started hastily to regain the boat. To their amazement they now saw that the iceberg, which they had thought securely grounded, had passed out between the capes on the ebbing tide. It had turned partially around, so that the platform on which their friends had stood was hidden by the Sphinx-like knob.

Ralph and Phil instantly realized the responsibility thus suddenly thrust upon them. With one accord they rushed down the rocks at imminent risk of a fall, jumped into the boat, and pushed off to the rescue. The iceberg was not so very far away even now, but it was clear, as soon as they caught the full force of the wind and waves, that the mass of ice, ponderous and slow-moving though it was, had most of the advantage in the race. It was affected far more by the powerful tidal current

Andy and Malcolm on the iceberg.   (*Page* 94.)

surging against its great submerged bulk than by
the wind which caught its exposed parts. The boat,
on the other hand, was hindered more by the wind
than it was helped by the current, and a choppy
sea added to the difficulty of rowing. The lads
pulled with desperation, but after a quarter of an
hour of it they had to admit that they were being
outstripped. They soon noticed that as the berg
increased its distance from the coast, the strength
of the tidal current flowing out of the harbor was
gradually spent, and the steady Labrador current
outside bent the iceberg's course southward.

TO Malcolm and Andy the situation in which they found themselves was trying indeed. Eastward they saw only tossing waters and distant icebergs. Westward near the shore there might be fishermen, but the turning of the berg prevented any attempt to attract their notice. There appeared no safe passage between the ledge and the opposite side of the berg, since the higher portions of the ice rose in an almost vertical wall behind the ledge, and where the wall did not block them the pond did.

This pond was no inconsiderable element of danger. It was not a shallow pool formed by the melting of the ice, but a basin of salt water maintaining the level of the sea and disturbed by the outer waves. Evidently, between the pond and the sea the ledge was badly fissured below, and the rushing of the water back and forth through the openings would soon cause its fall at that point. Where the cameras stood the ledge undoubtedly derived some support from the high wall at its rear.

The icy sides of the basin, about six feet high, were vertical and glare, and had one of the lads slipped in, the other would have found it almost impossible to render assistance. Nevertheless, Malcolm deemed it necessary to venture cautiously, boat-hook in hand, along the ledge to see if he could reach the shoreward side around the base of the Sphinx. He found that the ledge was terminated in that direction by an ice-cliff. Indeed he had hardly expected anything else, for he remembered how precipitous that side had seemed when he viewed it from the boat.

"It's no use," said he, when he returned. "I don't see that we can do a thing but wait for those two youngsters. They'll surely put out after us, but if this wind should be too strong for them we'll be in for quite a cruise, I'm thinking."

"Yes, if the berg will only hold together," said Andy, reassured by Malcolm's effort at cheerfulness. "It can't sink, anyhow. That's one comfort."

"Whatever happens," Malcolm remarked, "we must hang on to that boat-hook. It's indispensable when you're dealing with icebergs. By the way, couldn't we cut some footholds in this wall with it, and so climb up to the top? We could rig a signal of distress if we could only get up there."

"Come on," said Andy. "Let's try it."

They fell eagerly to work, Malcolm jabbing with the boat-hook and Andy hacking with his knife a little higher. Two steps were thus fashioned in the almost vertical wall. Then two more were cut above them. The boat-hook could now be used only at an ineffective angle, so the two took turns at standing in the steps already cut, and chipping out others. Gradually they worked up along the face of the dazzling cliff, bearing off a little toward the right to escape an overhanging part. This course brought them over the pond, where extreme caution was necessary. The steps were purposely sloped downward at the back so as to afford the feet a sure hold, and the lads took time enough to work thoroughly and carefully, impatient though they were to look over the top of the barrier.

There remained but three or four steps to be cut when Andy, who was below, shouted up to Malcolm that he could hear voices. Malcolm, intent on his task, had heard nothing, and was inclined to think that Andy's imagination had misled him or that he had heard some sea-bird. Andy, however, was positive, and a moment later he pointed triumphantly toward the far end of the berg, around which was slowly creeping against wind and sea the Viola's lifeboat. Ralph and Phil were tugging at the oars with all their strength to reach the windward side of the ice. They could not even pause to look for Malcolm and Andy, but the latter lost no time in reassuring them by shouts of encouragement. Malcolm came down from his perch with all possible speed and joined Andy on the ledge.

"Keep her off, keep her off," cautioned Malcolm. "Don't come round till you're well to windward, or you'll be blown against the berg. Hold her twenty feet out if you can. We've got to be careful not to swamp her."

The principal reason for his anxiety lay in the fact, already mentioned, that the sea had worn away the ice at the water-level, leaving a projecting rim at the height of about three feet along the front of the ledge. The big waves of the open ocean, as they dashed into this hollow, entirely filled it, and the spray, which otherwise would have drenched Malcolm and Andy, was thrown back in a horizontal direction. If the stern of the boat were caught under this rim upon the advance of a wave, the craft would be likely to fill instantly; and though her reservoirs of air might keep her from sinking, the boys had no mind to try that kind of experiment. The problem was, therefore, to let the wind drive her close enough to effect a rescue, and at the same time keep the stern free. Even if Ralph and Phil had seamanship enough for this, Malcolm feared their strength might be too far gone. He accordingly decided upon a plan which would put no risk upon any one but himself.

"Let her drift in closer now, boys," he called. Then, turning to Andy, he said in a low tone, "I'll have to go first in order to handle the boat. Give me the boat-hook, and be ready to do as I tell you."

To Andy, unused to rough-water boating, it seemed utterly reckless to try to gain the tossing craft from the slippery, sloping edge of the ice. But he had great faith in Malcolm, so he passed the boat-hook over and waited to see what the young sailor would do.

The boat was being forced toward the ice, though its valiant crew took care to resist the power of the wind to some extent. When the stern was within five feet of the berg, Malcolm commanded, "Hold her now — hold her right there as steady as you can." Then poising the boat-hook before him and watching the boat intently as it rose and fell, he

suddenly drove the point of the spike into the ice
where the downward slope began, and using the
shaft as a vaulting-pole he launched himself out
over the interval of water with a nicely calculated
spring. He landed safely just within the stern.
But there was no time to lose.

"Quick! Give me your oars, Phil," he cried.
"I'll take care of the boat. Ralph, you fend off
with the boat-hook if we strike. Phil, stand aft and
take the cameras from Andy."

As the instruments were still attached to their
tripods, Andy was enabled to hold them out within
reach of Phil. And now it only remained to take
off Andy himself.

"Will you vault or slide?" called Malcolm.

"I guess I can get there with just a plain jump,"
answered Andy, "that is, if you can come a little
closer."

"How's that, then?" Malcolm had allowed the
stern to slip into the cleft where the rim was not
so pronounced, but hardly had he spoken when the
bow dipped and the stern rose so that the boat
was tilted quite away from the berg, and Andy
hesitated.

"I wish she'd stay still half a second," said he.

"Just watch the waves," counselled Malcolm,

" and jump when the stern 's going down. Give him
sea-room there, Phil."

" All right," said Phil. " Come on." And Andy,
watching his chance, presently came. He miscalculated by several inches, and smashed a seat, but
fortunately did not injure himself.

Malcolm and Andy now took the oars, while
Ralph and Phil, after resuming their oilskin suits
so as to prevent too rapid cooling, settled themselves
in the stern as passengers. It was past noon, and
the pangs of hunger were making themselves felt.
Hence a direct course was laid for the mouth of the
harbor. Meantime the two rescuers, in response to
many questions, told how they had succeeded in
overtaking the runaway berg. When they first
reached the open sea they had indeed despaired of
making much progress. But that proved the hardest
and most discouraging part of the struggle. Ralph
was confident that if they could once get well out
from the shore they could head a little west of south
and then the wind would help them. This they did,
and no sooner had they changed the course than it
became a comparatively easy matter to make up
the distance which they had lost, and to gain upon
the berg. Three times it was necessary to beat to the
eastward for a few minutes, but their speed in a

southerly direction averaged better than that of the ice-mass after they were fairly out in the open.

" You could hardly have stood it," declared Malcolm, " if you had n't shovelled that coal. That was what hardened your muscles and stiffened your backs. We 're mightily obliged to you and proud of you, — Andy and I, — eh, Andy? It was a good piece of work."

" That it was," said Andy, heartily.

Now came the question of dinner. It was agreed that they should land in the first sheltered cove within the entrance, build a fire, and sample Caesar's provisions. A suitable place being found, all set to work to collect dry driftwood. Then in the lee of high rocks, by the genial warmth of the blaze, they feasted.

The meal finished, they decided to return to the ship. Not a shot had they fired, nor indeed had they seen any game-birds or animals. True, a seal or two had been sighted among the outer rocks, but to have killed these would have been wanton destruction, — a kind of sport in which none of the four cared to indulge. As to making a more serious effort at hunting, the consensus of opinion seemed to be that they had all had exercise and adventure enough for one day.

" There 's just one thing I 'm sorry we did n't get," said Andy, on the way up the harbor.

" For instance," said Ralph, persuasively.

" I wish Phil had taken a picture of that iceberg with us on it. Would n't it make my mother open her eyes! "

" Maybe I did," said Phil, with an air of mystery.

" How? From the rocks, when you went after that cap? But you could n't. Your camera was on the berg."

" I was n't going to tell you about that," answered Phil, " till I could surprise you with the picture itself. I stowed a hand-camera that I found on the Viola in the bow of this boat for instantaneous pictures. I was n't quite used to it, but I snapped it at you as we were pulling away from the berg, so maybe you 'll have your wish."

As they came within hailing distance of the steamer, they saw the Captain and Henry watching them, and Malcolm, for one, felt tolerably certain that he would be held to account for the escapade. This opinion was not at all shaken when the Captain sang out, " Do you know what I 've a mind to do with you boys? Put you in irons and diet you on hardtack and salt water."

It is true that this appeared to generalize the

responsibility, but Malcolm had already resolved to shoulder it all, come what would. He was not surprised that his father seemed to know the whole story, for they could easily have been seen from the Viola as they stood upon the ice. Arrived on deck, he pleaded guilty at once, and acknowledged that the project of boarding the berg was an imprudent one, and the fault was his. But his companions stood by him loyally. They stoutly maintained that they were the real culprits, and they told how Malcolm had tried to discourage them. The outcome was that the Captain let them all off with some sound advice on the folly of approaching an iceberg, especially a weather-worn one, in a small boat. Probably the memory of the Viola's recent disastrous approach to one, even though under different circumstances, was more or less a factor in his leniency.

CHAPTER IX

FLOE–ICE AND FOG

DURING Sunday, the following day, there were signs that the clouds would soon disperse. The little crew were now refreshed and ready to continue the voyage, though they well knew that the hardest part was before them. To cross Davis Strait from their present position would require, under the most favorable circumstances, considerably more time than they had consumed between Bacalieu and Cape Charles, and they all understood that their strength and endurance would be taxed to the utmost. But the thought that they might be able to save many lives spurred them on. Even Caesar appeared reconciled to departure.

That night the stars were seen, and by sunrise a fair day was assured by wind, weather, and barometer, alike. The former routine of work was again instituted, steam was made, and the Viola passed out between the capes and headed northeast. She crossed the zone of icebergs that day, and during the next two no ice of any description was seen.

Nothing broke the calm expanse of blue except a floating log which they sighted on the third day out. This log, Captain Ayre said, came from Siberia on the current setting southward along the east coast of Greenland.

At breakfast time on Thursday, in latitude 61° by dead reckoning, floe-ice was discovered ahead. This consisted of small, scattered, and much worn pieces, the remains of some great ice-field. It must have drifted around Cape Farewell from the east coast, like the Siberian log. The sky was cloudy, and to the eastward was a marked ice-blink — the luminous reflection in the heavens from ice beneath. The boys had noticed a like luminosity, though on a smaller scale, denoting the position of icebergs that lay just beneath the horizon.

Perceiving this long ice-blink, Captain Ayre surmised that there was no passage in that direction. In the extreme north was a dark, open-water sky, but after approaching the floe in that quarter for about an hour and finding it more dense, the steamer headed westward and southward in an endeavor to go around the pack. Later the fog closed in, and the Viola lay off and on at slow speed, while the Captain and Henry, leaving Malcolm in charge, turned in for a wink of sleep.

The atmosphere clearing in the night, Malcolm called up captain and engineer, and the Viola once more skirted the field of ice-pans. The voyagers were now so far north that the nights were not absolutely dark at any hour. Dusk did not arrive until late, and the dawn was early in evidence. Hence the dangers of navigation at night were reduced to a minimum.

Andy and Ralph, waking after four hours of sleep, looked out through their port-hole on that Arctic sea and felt strangely far from home. No ice was in sight on that side of the ship, and the Viola was bowling along merrily. They rose, donned their working clothes again, and went on deck. It was cold, but the air was delicious. The mercury stood at 37° — almost down to the freezing point — in a thermometer on the upper deck. Captain Ayre was at the wheel, Malcolm having gone below to rest.

" Good-morning, lads," said the Captain, cheerily. " If you 'll look over yonder I think you 'll see something you never saw before." He pointed to the east.

Andy and Ralph made out several purple and white patches above the grayness of the far horizon. Was it land? For a few moments they were not sure. It might be an effect of clouds. They asked the Captain about it, but he only said, "Watch."

Presently the clouds were distinguished by their motion, while the purple peaks remained. Yes, they were looking for the first time on Greenland, the land of their dreams and hopes. It seemed truly an enchanted place — a coast that might just be glimpsed afar off amid ice and fog, but never reached. Soon the mists had blotted it from sight.

"Those must have been high mountains," said Andy. "What part of Greenland was it?"

"That highest peak was probably Mt. Nautsarsorfik," answered the Captain. "It is marked on the chart as having an altitude of 5240 feet, and is south of the settlement of Frederikshaab. No doubt it is as much as forty-five miles distant from us. There's ice in that direction, and we have a good many miles northing to make, so I shall not head in for the land just yet."

Andy and Ralph now hastened to relieve Henry and Phil in the fire-room. On the way thither they surprised Caesar, who was getting breakfast, with the announcement that they had seen Greenland.

"Laws a massy!" cried the delighted cook. "Is we really got dar? Why, I ain' froze ma ears, or felt any 'markable 'frigeration ob de atmosphere.

I ain' gwine b'lieve dese yer Artic trabblers no mo'.' "

" Perhaps it 's colder in winter," suggested Ralph.

" Mebbe dat 's so, but de summer am sholy bery respec'able."

Henry and Phil were no less pleased when they heard the news, and they too must needs strain their eyes eastward before going, the one to the engines, and the other to his bunk.

A little later, while still holding a northerly course, the steamer ran into pack-ice again, and was guided between the pans at full speed, since she answered her wheel more accurately and promptly so than she would have done at a more leisurely pace.   Captain Ayre was skilful at this kind of piloting, seeming to know by instinct those passages which were wide enough.   But once or twice a mass of a few tons' weight was struck a glancing blow and pushed to one side.   Such pieces might cause trouble, so at length the speed was reduced and the course changed to southwest.   Before the Viola had run out of the floe the mists were upon her again, and it became necessary to stop all headway.

During the afternoon the fog dissolved, and it was possible to proceed slowly in a westerly direction.   To starboard the dazzling floe extended as far as the eye could reach, and hour after hour they skirted that unbroken barrier. Here and there an iceberg pierced the white field. Brightly shone the August sun, but it imparted little warmth, for even midsummer breezes are chill in the Davis Strait.

Not till late evening, when the tardy northern dusk came creeping faintly upon the sky and sea, was there a change in the situation. Now the white line far ahead is seen to be broken. A dark water-way leads northward through the ice. Malcolm, muffled to the chin, climbs to the foretop, and soon from that airy lookout shouts welcome news to his friends on the bridge. Not only is the passage amply wide, but away beyond the pack he can see open water. The Viola is headed for the "lead" and shortly enters the tortuous channel.

It is a scene of typical Arctic beauty, and the young stokers take turns in running up on deck to view it. Ahead lies a bewildering labyrinth of sombre waterways and glittering spires, into whose icy grottoes the sea hurls itself with splash and sullen roar. On either hand the ice-field stretches away into the softening twilight. Every cavern and crevice among the floating masses is tinted deeply blue, while the fantastic pinnacles that rise above the general level are snow-white and well set off

against the dark canals. Now and then a seal is
distinguished, lying like a black log flat upon the
ice or making clumsy efforts to reach the water.
Into this weird scene of solitude the ship makes
her way bravely, silently — the one touch of living
human interest that completes the picture.

Alternate fog and sunshine characterized the following day, the mercury standing at 34°. The wind
remained so light as to be scarcely perceptible, and
the sea barely rippled. At noon Captain Ayre determined his position to be latitude 62° 50′, longitude
53° 49′. Early in the day some ice was seen, and
more in the afternoon and evening, including one
large iceberg.

Sunday, the next day, was as monotonous as only
an Arctic fog could make it. Pack-ice beset the
Viola again on all sides and progress was impossible,
though the Captain declared that if he were on his
own sealing steamer he could push straight through
the floes. Many times he was heard to exclaim upon
the folly of the Viola's people in deliberately taking
an iron ship into such waters. The Captain would
take no more chances here than were absolutely
necessary. He could hardly have bettered the situation by proceeding even slowly, for it was possible
to see but little farther than a ship's length, and

out of that gray mist there came an incessant roaring. Not far away the floe was probably denser, and the cakes were grinding together as they rocked upon the long swells. Perhaps, too, the sound of surf upon the floe-edge or upon icebergs had a part in that mysterious sound. The little crew of the Viola could not know. They could only listen and wonder what was hidden over yonder.

All day a flock of great gray birds — pomarine jaegers, Malcolm said they were — flew or floated about the steamer. Ralph desired to stuff and mount a specimen or two, and hit upon a unique method of capturing them. He appeared on the after-deck with a long line having a hook on the end of it baited with corned beef and floated by a cork. This he flung far out astern, and presently one of the jaegers paddled up to it and swallowed the tempting morsel. Then the line was slowly drawn in, pulling the big bird along in the water toward the ship in spite of himself. For the last fifty feet he flew, and so, guided by the line, he came at last over the rail and fairly into the arms of his captor.

The fog continued until Monday afternoon, but grew more diaphanous, so that slow speed was possible. At noon a sounding gave no bottom in one hundred fathoms. Late in the day, when the lower

8

air cleared and most of the ice had disappeared, full speed was resumed until the slowly gathering darkness — for the night was cloudy — made it unsafe. It was now a week since the steamer had left Cape Charles, and it seemed as if the greater part of that precious time had been wasted among ice-floes. Yet without those opportunities for rest the prize crew would have been worn out. Tuesday morning, August 7, they rejoiced to find the Greenland coast in plain sight, with no ice intervening.

CHAPTER X

PROFESSOR ROTH'S STORY

IT was a dark, mountainous coast there to the eastward, and might have been ten miles distant. Heavy mists obscured the peaks and so changed the aspect of the country that for some hours Captain Ayre could not obtain any clue to his exact position. He had lost his reckoning in the ice-floes and fogs. Cautiously, therefore, the steamer drew in closer, plying back and forth and blowing her whistle at intervals to attract the attention of the inhabitants, if there were any.

At length the mists lifted a little, discovering a prominent double-peaked mountain which the Captain recognized upon the chart.

"It's the Sugar Loaves," said he to Malcolm and Phil, who were then off duty. "This is the very spot we were looking for. There's a settlement over in there called Sukkertoppen — I suppose that's Danish for Sugar Loaves — or rather New Sukkertoppen, for there's an Old Sukkertoppen some miles north. The two villages evidently take their name from the mountain. They 've certainly got a good landmark. The Eskimo name òn the chart is Manitsok."

The identity of the coast he speedily communicated to Henry through the tube, while Malcolm and Phil hastened below to tell Caesar and Andy and Ralph, all of whom were in the fire-room.

By the aid of a glass, one little house was seen near the water's edge, and there were flagstaffs on several rocky elevations, but as yet no other signs of life appeared. Malcolm now sent up an explosive rocket from the upper deck, the Captain having no mind to run in too far upon such a forbidding shore without a pilot. But after lying on and off for what seemed a long time without perceiving any activity landward, he was on the point of heading north along the coast when Phil, who had returned and picked up the glass, exclaimed excitedly, " They 're coming! I can see a canoe."

" Ah! let me look," said the Captain. He took the glass and poised it steadily. " Yes, you 're right, Phil. That 's a kayak, the native skin-canoe. There are three or four more astern of her. We shall know pretty soon now whether Professor Roth's people are here or not." He signalled to Henry to stop the engines.

The kayak is a very small craft for the open ocean, and holds but one man. Those that were approaching the Viola could at first barely be discerned as little black specks when they rose on the crests of the waves. As they came nearer, each Eskimo was seen to be paddling swiftly with a double-bladed paddle, and balancing himself with wonderful dexterity as he sat in the little round cockpit.

In due time these swarthy fellows made their kayaks fast to the ladder, tucked their paddles under a taut seal-hide thong, and clambered on board the steamer, where they looked about them with wide-eyed astonishment and pleasure. Even the engineer and his three stokers left their posts for a moment upon the arrival of these interesting people, and the two parties stared curiously at each other for some seconds. Then Malcolm made signs that the Eskimos should accompany him to the pilot-house, where the Captain put them through a series of questions by a mixture of words and signs. Replying in like manner, they were able to convey the information quite clearly that there was a harbor with deep water, that the place was New Sukkertoppen, and that there were " plenty men." By this last the Captain understood them to mean the people of the Viola.

Under the guidance of the Eskimos the steamer was headed shoreward. She was soon met by a whaleboat containing several Eskimos, a Danish pilot, and Professor Roth himself. Captain Ayre at once turned over the ship to the pilot and invited the Professor into the engine-room, in order that Henry might talk with him also.

The Professor was a light-complexioned man of medium height and weight, and evidently of German ancestry. He hastened to express his unbounded surprise at finding that the steamer was in reality the Viola, which he and his party had given up for lost.

" This is almost too good to be true! " cried he, as he took the chair which Henry offered. His face was fairly beaming. " May I ask, gentlemen, to whom I am indebted for this great service ? "

" This is Captain Ayre, of St. John's, Newfoundland," answered Henry. " My name is Hollister. We were camping on the Newfoundland coast, and discovered the Viola drifting upon an outlying island on the twenty-second of July."

" You don't say so! She did a bit of travelling on her own account, did n't she ? Was she damaged ? "

" Not in the least."

" I thought you had patched up her bow, by the looks of it."

" True, but we ourselves are responsible for that hole. We bumped her into an iceberg in the fog near Belle Isle."

" Ah! But without spoiling her seaworthiness. That was fortunate. How many men have you, Mr. Hollister ? "

" Well," said Henry, smiling, " that depends somewhat on where you draw the line. Phil Schuyler, our youngest, is fourteen years old. My brother Ralph is sixteen. Andy Faxon is seventeen, I believe. Malcolm, the Captain's son, is eighteen. Then there are the Captain here, and Caesar the cook, and myself, — seven all told. But there is n't one, Professor, who has n't done a man's work aboard this craft."

" I can well believe that," said the Professor, " if you mean to tell me that you seven have brought this steamer all the way from Newfoundland."

" That 's the truth," said the Captain, " and I 'm proud of my crew. But tell us, Professor, are your people all safe ? And how came you to abandon the ship ? "

" They are all safe. As to your second question, it happened in this wise. We negotiated from New

York for a sealing steamer to carry our expedition, but at the last moment the negotiations fell through, and we were forced to abandon the enterprise or charter this iron vessel. We chose the latter course, though we knew she was not built for Arctic service. However, we reasoned that in the summer there would be no need of forcing her into ice-floes, and we could work along the coast during intervals of fair weather, exploring, hunting, making scientific collections, and taking photographs, and so possibly go as far north as Peary's headquarters.

"We made the mistake of starting too early. The ice-floes were not much softened or broken up when we encountered them, and we were caught by the shifting pack almost before we realized that there was danger. Several times we were able to go forward for half a day or less, but we could n't escape to open waters. Finally the floes closed in upon us more tightly than ever. It was then that we feared for the safety of the ship, for the ice began piling up against her sides, and we knew her unbraced iron hull would n't stand much pressure. Under these circumstances, when the barometer commenced to fall rapidly and a severe storm seemed imminent, our captain advised that the passengers and crew cross the ice to the coast, which was only four miles away, taking with them as large a supply of provisions as possible. If the steamer survived the storm and remained where she was, it might then be feasible to board her again; but if she was crushed and went down, we should at least be safe for the time being.

" This was decided to be the prudent course. We therefore made a number of sledges and put three weeks' provisions on them and started over the ice, first taking the precaution to leave a note in a bottle on the upper deck, in case the steamer should go adrift but survive. I judge you found that note, gentlemen."

" We did," said the Captain.

" We had hardly covered two of the four miles," continued the Professor, " when the expected storm broke, and we saw that we could bring no more provisions out of the ship. As it was, we were fortunate to get to the rocks with what we had, for it was an offshore gale, and the ice, soon after we left it, began to break up and move seaward. It took the Viola with it, and we lost sight of her in the blur of mist and rain.

" Our situation then was one of extreme discomfort. We had a few tents, but not enough for more than half the passengers, not to mention the crew. We did not know just where we were, and had no boats with which to explore. Our food supply was good so far as it went, but there was no fuel for cooking after we had broken and burned the sledges and what little driftwood lay among the rocks. We thought we might possibly hold out for four or five weeks, with the help of our firearms, but it looked as if the end must come sooner or later.

" The gale blew for four days and made us all thoroughly miserable. We were drenched and cold, and very blue over the loss of our ship, but on the fifth day we were discovered by a native in a kayak. From him we learned that we were on a large island, on the other side of which was the settlement of Sukkertoppen. The Eskimo returned to the village for help and came back with the Danish Inspector's whaleboat. In this, in the course of several trips, we were all transported to Sukker-toppen, together with our supplies, and were given comfortable quarters in the Government storehouses. From Sukkertoppen as a base of operations, our scientists have gone out to explore the fiords and glaciers of the neighboring mainland, and the sportsmen have organized numerous hunting trips. There are only a few of our people actually in the village at this time. They'll be rather surprised, I fancy,

Exploring the glacier. (*Page* 122.)

when they recognize the Viola," and the Professor rubbed his hands together gleefully.

Captain Ayre now excused himself, saying that he had left Malcolm in the wheelhouse to assist the pilot, but that perhaps he ought to be there himself, for they must be nearing the harbor. Even as he turned away, the signal rang for slow speed.

" Well, Professor, you 've certainly had quite a little adventure," said Henry, as he grasped the controlling levers. " I suppose now you will continue your voyage northward."

" I think so. And you and all your party must come along as our guests. Promise me that, Mr. Hollister."

" Thank you, we shall be delighted. Those boys, I 'm sure, will be very much tickled at the thought of going on, provided the coal is shovelled by some one else. I rather suspect they 've had enough of stoking."

" I should think so too," said the Professor. " They deserve gold medals. If you have no objection I shall get the regular crew aboard and relieve you at the earliest possible moment. You must be about worn out."

" A little rest and sleep won't do us any harm," Henry admitted. " Still, we 're not in bad shape.

We could stand it another fortnight if we had to."

The Viola had now rounded a rocky elevation and was entering the harbor, at the head of which lay the village. Behind its whitewashed buildings was a precipitous ridge, perhaps two hundred feet high, which rose at the right into domes of somewhat greater altitude. The anchorage was well sheltered on all sides, but so small that it could not have accommodated many steamships at one time. Nor was there need, for it was probable that never in the history of the place had more than two been there together.

Before she reached the entrance the Viola had been recognized by her crew, who set up a great cheer and then put off to her with Captain Barrett and the other officers in such miscellaneous boats as were at hand. As soon as they came on board, Captain Barrett went to the bridge, two Swedish stokers were sent to the fire-room to relieve Caesar and Phil, Henry turned over his charge to the engineers, while the second officer with the boatswain and two seamen went forward to be ready to drop the port anchor, and others of the crew prepared the cables which were to be stretched to ringbolts in the rocks as an additional safeguard. The little prize crew's work was done, and each member of it was heartily glad to be freed from further toil and responsibility.

As soon as they had means of transportation, ten or twelve of the Viola's passengers also came out to her. These included the more elderly and some who had joined the expedition as tourists or seekers after health. They did not desire or were not able to take part in the scientific and hunting trips, and hence had remained quietly in the settlement. Needless to say, they were eager to make the acquaintance of Captain Ayre and his " men," and to hear the story of the saving of the steamer. When they had heard it, nothing would do but that their rescuers should share with them in everything. Firearms, cameras, field-glasses, and other valuables were urged upon each one, but were politely refused. Henry's party was already fairly well supplied with such things, and, beside, it seemed in better taste to take no valuable rewards. The only articles which the boys decided to accept were ribbons, knives, and trinkets suitable for trading on a small scale with the natives.

CHAPTER XI

SUKKERTOPPEN AND THE ESKIMOS

C APTAIN AYRE and Henry gave the boys absolute freedom as soon as the regular crew arrived, and in their eagerness to go ashore the four could hardly wait to put off their grimy garments and comb the coal-dust out of their hair. When this was accomplished and their faces shone with vigorous scrubbings, a dory was launched, and they set forth, — Phil with his camera, Ralph with his botanist's case, and all with a supply of trading material. A landing was made on the nearest smooth rocks, though they afterward learned that there was a little wharf in an inlet at the rear of the village.

Two or three Eskimo men who appeared to have nothing to do were the only natives in sight, and they nodded a welcome. The boys conjectured that most of the men were absent with the Viola's people.

Proceeding a short distance along a shell path, they saw before them a flagstaff flying the red and white emblem of Denmark. For the first time in their lives they stood on Danish soil. But what interested them even more was the sight which was presented at the foot of the flagstaff. Here were grouped apparently all the women and children in the settlement. With the very best of manners, they had not flocked down to the shore to crowd around as the boys landed, but had stationed themselves picturesquely at this point, where they could see the new-comers as they approached the Inspector's house. Phil fairly gasped with delight. Here was a most unique picture all ready to be taken. He took his stand instantly in front of the group, set up the camera, and raised his hand as a signal that all should keep still. Every woman and child, and even the babies, seemed to understand. They were as immovable as statues. But at the first attempt Phil forgot a very important part of the operation, — that of drawing the slide to expose the plate, — nor did he notice the omission until Andy, his own pupil in photography, burst out laughing.

"Well, I certainly did get rattled that time," said Phil, with good grace. "I'll try again." And he did, with better success.

The costumes of the natives seemed extremely

novel to the boys. The men wore jackets made whole like a sweater, with eider-down or fur inside and calico on the outside. Attached was a hood, which, most of the time, was thrown back from their luxuriant black locks. Some of the men wore trousers made from the hide of the hair-seal, but the majority of them had obtained cloth garments in trade from fishermen. They wore soft boots called kamiks, of sealskin, reaching just above the ankle, the hair being inside except an ornamental strip around the top.

The women wore jackets much like those of the men, but the remainder of their clothing was different. Their boots reached just above the knee, and were of seal leather dyed red, blue, brown, or white. The boots, unless white, were ingeniously ornamented by two strips of white leather sewn from the toe to the knee, where they branched like the prongs of a fork. Around the tops were bands of white leather and fur. The trousers of the women came to the knees and fitted into the boots. Unlike the boots, the trousers had the seal-hair outside, but were likewise adorned with two vertical strips of white leather. In some instances beautiful necklaces of colored beads were displayed. These were so wide as to cover the breast and shoulders. Babies were carried in a sort of hood on their mothers' backs.

Red bandannas seemed much in vogue as head-dresses, yet these were not worn so universally as the band of ribbon which denoted the state of each woman. The hair was drawn tightly back into a tuft or roll, and around this the ribbon was wound. Red was for the maiden, blue for the wife, and black for the widow. If a widow was willing to marry again, she coyly mingled some red with the sombre hue of mourning.

The house of the Inspector, or Governor of the district, was close at hand. It was a square, two-storied wooden cottage, painted black, but with white window-frames enclosing very small panes of glass, six to a window. A single chimney sur-mounted the centre of the shingled roof. Around the house a small plot had been levelled and covered with sand and shell, and this was enclosed with a neat picket fence. In this yard the boys were sur-prised to see croquet wickets. Several chickens were scratching for a livelihood, though angle-worms must have been scarce indeed. There were also two or three dogs, but not of the real Eskimo breed.

Proceeding toward the house, the boys received a most hospitable welcome from Mrs. Bistrup, wife

9

of the Inspector, the latter, as they learned, being
away on a visit to a neighboring settlement. Their
young son and daughter, with Assistant-Inspector
Baumann and wife, and Miss Fausboll, daughter
of Professor Fausboll of the University of Copenhagen, were also at the house and assisted in their
entertainment. Miss Fausboll was a niece of Mrs.
Bistrup, and had come on the mail steamer to spend
the winter with her. Very fortunately all three of
the ladies spoke excellent English, and the young
Americans were made to feel quite at home. In
the cozy library they told the story of the finding
of the Viola to an interested audience, and though
they had little to say about their achievement in
bringing the steamer to Greenland, the ladies drew
them out somewhat and declared that they had
performed wonders.

The Inspector's was a well-furnished home. The
parlor contained beautiful fur rugs and handsome
furniture. There was a piano, and what was
Ralph's surprise to discover the music and Danish
translation of " After the Ball." Truly a popular
song goes to the ends of the earth. In the book-
case, among other works, they noticed a set of
Dickens in Danish. Tasteful pictures adorned the
walls, and in the window bloomed geraniums, chrys-

anthemums, and mignonette. It was a home such as one would hardly expect to find in Greenland.

From their Danish friends the boys gathered several interesting items. Mr. Baumann told them that there was but one cat in all Greenland. It was at Godthaab, the nearest settlement on the south. These animals do not thrive in such a severe climate.

In explaining the scarcity of dogs at Sukker-toppen, Mrs. Bistrup said that they had all died of a plague, and there were no full-grown ones nearer than Holsteinborg. She also referred to a sickness which had carried off about fifteen persons at Sukkertoppen some years before, saying that they had died of an *epitome;* but when her niece asked if she did not mean an epidemic, she laughingly accepted the amendment and declared she would have to renew the study of English. But the boys thought she succeeded remarkably well, especially as the unexpected arrival of the expedition had given her no time for refreshing her memory. She said that consumption was prevalent among the natives, having been introduced by the white people. It had spread easily, owing to the unsanitary ways of the Eskimos.

The advent of the Viola's party had been a great piece of good luck to Mrs. Baumann, who had dreaded the long journey to Copenhagen, which she felt must soon be made for the purpose of consulting a dentist. There happened to be a dentist from New York in the stranded party, and he, on learning of the contemplated trip, offered his services. They were gratefully accepted, the work was done, and the perils and discomforts of the long voyage averted. After that, nothing was too good for the dentist, and he was the recipient of many fine gifts, including a beautiful model of a kayak specially made for the Inspector.

The houses of the natives were, of course, far less pretentious, as the boys discovered on continuing their explorations. They were small, ill-lighted, and damp, built of stones, and covered and chinked with turf green and growing. A few had a wooden superstructure and roof, but wood is not easily procurable in that country, and the natives cannot afford to use it lavishly.

Piles of refuse, containing fish-bones and the remains of seals, gave the Eskimo portion of the settlement a disagreeable odor, but no one seemed to mind it. " I suppose," said Andy, " this smell is just as pleasant to them as the fragrance of apple-blossoms is to us. It has a connection in their minds with food."

"Is that why you like the smell of apple-blossoms?" asked Ralph, pretending that his esthetic sensibilities had received a shock.

"Well," answered Andy, "perhaps that is n't the whole reason, but I certainly do like apples, and I'm sure these people like blubber."

There were thirty or forty houses and huts in the place, and a population of perhaps three hundred, the Danes numbering less than a dozen. But there is more or less white blood in all these South Greenland natives, and many of them, if the dirt were removed, would hardly be darker than a European. Occasionally one was met who had the oblique eyes, prominent cheek-bones, and olive complexion of the true Mongolian, but only far to the north could one be sure of seeing pure-blooded Eskimos.

The interior of a native hut which the four entered after stooping through a low passageway furnished many surprises. On the walls were cartoons from "Puck" and "Judge" and various Danish papers, and quaint old chromos and prints, all of which had been obtained from sailors or the Danes. The furniture was of the rudest description, consisting of a wooden bench, a set of board shelves, and a platform, also of boards, which extended across one end of the apartment and was doubtless

the family bedstead, as it was piled high with eider-
down quilts more or less greasy and crumpled. A
rusty little stove proclaimed the occupants of that
hut somewhat better off in the social scale than the
majority of their neighbors. For fuel they used peat
or dried roots, though the boys did not doubt that
in winter they relied upon oil. There was a strong
smell of fish and oil in the hut, but it was not as
bad as they had expected from the stories they had
read.

In addition to the houses of the Inspector and the
Assistant-Inspector, the Danish Government had
built a number of storehouses and outbuildings of
various sizes. These were all of stone neatly painted
white, and had sloping shingled roofs. Around one
of the largest were a great many empty oil barrels,
showing the use to which that building was put.
There was a little store which was open two hours
daily for the sale of cloth and other articles needed
by the natives.

Malcolm learned that the Government bought up
all the white bear and blue fox skins, walrus ivory,
and seal oil, and that the Greenlanders were not
allowed to trade away these commodities. Apparently, therefore, a rising hope on the part of the
boys of obtaining furs and ivory from the Eskimos

was not to be realized, but they still thought the dream might materialize with the aid of their own rifles when they reached Melville Bay. In that frigid region they could unquestionably shoot walruses and polar bears to their hearts' content.

Andy made inquiries as to the hunting and fishing in the neighborhood of Sukkertoppen, and was told that reindeer could be found about forty miles inland. The hair-seal was of course common, but had no particular value to the boys. There were codfish and halibut along the coast, and salmon-trout in the lakes and rivers.

Phil had not been long on shore when he decided to see what kind of trading the natives would do. By this time most of the women and children had dispersed to their habitations, and those of the men who had not gone away with Inspector Bistrup or the Viola's parties were also to be found in the native portion of the village. So Phil, starting off by himself, took a path which led over the rocks in that direction and terminated at the church. It was the only highway in the place except the paths to the landings. Among the rocks on each side were patches of the rich green grass which springs up with exceeding luxuriance in the Greenland villages because the scant soil has been fertilized for generations by the remains of fish and seals.

Perceiving a group of Eskimo women before him in the path, he bethought him of some little round looking-glasses which he had in his pockets. Here was a chance to determine whether the woman of Greenland would consider that article as indispensable to her boudoir as does her American cousin. Phil therefore produced a looking-glass and held it so that the nearest woman would see her own face in it. She appeared delighted, and wished to take the mirror in her hands, while the others crowded around, laughing merrily. Then Phil brought out a few more and imprudently handed them out among the group. He was not very particular as to what he should receive in trade for them, since any article of Eskimo manufacture would be a curiosity at home; so when one of the women offered him a sealskin purse and another a pair of baby's mittens, he accepted them. But when nothing further seemed forthcoming he began to gather in the looking-glasses from those who had done no trading.

And now he discovered that woman is, in truth, pretty much the same all over the world. The looking-glasses were treasures in the eyes of these Eskimo belles, and it was with evident reluctance that they surrendered them. Presently he found that he had all but one of those which were due, and made signs to indicate that he had missed it. Several of the women now began to titter, and one or two looked at him in a sidelong way precisely like a child that has done wrong. It was plain that the women had been passing the glass back and forth between them until one, by common agreement, could secrete it while Phil's back was turned. Which woman had it he could not quite determine. She might have slipped it up her sleeve or down her boot, — at any rate, it was in vain that he pointed threateningly toward the Inspector's house and continued his gestures. The looking-glass remained in its hiding-place, and Phil was forced to put it down to profit and loss.

On the whole, he did not regret this experience, for it gave him a sidelight on the Eskimo character. He had read that these natives were strictly honest if intrusted outright with any kind of property, but that they would sometimes steal if they could do it slyly under the eye of the owner. So, in the present instance, they knew he might have distributed fewer glasses and kept better account of them, and it was in the nature of a practical joke that one turned up missing. But as long as he was in Sukkertoppen there was one Eskimo woman who looked at Phil always with that childish, guilty-conscience expression, and he concluded that her fault would be its own sufficient punishment.

Passing on after the incident of the looking-glass, Phil came to the Lutheran Church, a much more pretentious building than that at Cape Charles Harbor, Labrador. The white walls were of painted stone to a height of twelve feet, where, on the sides, the sloping shingled roof came down to meet them. At the front was a low, pointed spire, surmounted by a cross, and built of wood shingled from the ground to the peak. The wood, of course, had been shipped from Denmark.

Near the church was a deep inlet. Turning in that direction, Phil discovered Andy paddling about in a kayak, while an old Eskimo stood on the shore watching him with the greatest amusement. Andy found the strange craft as difficult to balance as is a bicycle in the hands of a novice. The paddle was a single piece of wood bladed somewhat at each end. In a rough sea or in any emergency the Eskimos rely upon a quick stroke of this paddle to keep them upright, but as Andy was not skilled in its use he was in imminent danger of capsizing, or so it seemed to Phil. Hardly had the thought come into his mind when over went the kayak.

Phil was much alarmed, for the kayak was decked over with seal-hide except the snug, round cockpit, and his friend could not free himself. The canoe was bottom up, and its unfortunate navigator was head down in the icy water at least ten feet from shore. Phil glanced quickly at the old Eskimo to see what he would do, but that individual was still placidly smiling. Either he thought it was some strange trick of the white youth, or was waiting for the twist of the paddle which would bring him right-side up. But Andy had let the paddle go, for it rose to the surface and floated away. The next moment, however, by swimming with his hands, he managed to get his head above water, though he could not entirely right the kayak. He was strongly built and a powerful swimmer, and his exertions soon brought him within reach of Phil's outstretched hand. It is unnecessary to add that he lost no time in disembarking from the treacherous craft.

At this juncture Ralph and Malcolm came running up. Seeing Andy drenched but safe, they began to berate him jokingly for not waiting long enough to have his picture taken, swimming in a Greenland pool. Thereupon Andy, who could not be any wetter,

told Phil to set up the camera, and then, after
running about to keep his blood circulating, he
cheerfully jumped in again and swam around
for a few seconds, to the huge delight of the old
Eskimo. The water was too cold for much more
than a plunge, and he quickly climbed out with
chattering teeth and ran off toward the landing
and the ship.

Malcolm and Ralph and Phil returned more
leisurely, and made several trades. A ribbon pur-
chased an Eskimo doll dressed in complete native
garb. A pair of gloves and a looking-glass procured
a fine pair of woman's red kamiks. Fifty öre, or
about fourteen cents of American money, together
with a looking-glass and blue ribbon, were given for
a pair of blue kamiks. Fifty öre each was the
price of two bird-darts. Two kroner, or fifty-six
cents, bought a handsome pillow of eider-down, covered with variegated birdskins. Finally a little
fellow about eight years old came to Ralph and
offered a new seal-hide cap trimmed with soft gray
eider-down. Ralph thought he knew what would
please him, so he showed him a pocket-knife. At
sight of it the boy's eyes lighted up. He thrust the
cap into Ralph's hands, cried "Nuff," as he had
doubtless been instructed, grabbed the knife, and

ran off in high feather, while Ralph was not a whit less pleased, for the cap was a beauty.

After the boys had returned to the steamer an Eskimo came out in his kayak to offer a paddle in trade. He was met by one of the Viola's passengers, who, having heard that the natives are afflicted with snow-blindness at seasons when the sun is bright upon the snow, showed him a pair of dark glasses which are a good preventive of this malady. The Eskimo seemed pleased with the offer, and the bargain was made. But later in the day he returned with another native who repeated many times the words, "Him my brudder," and made signs that they wished to regain the paddle and return the dark glasses. The passenger, however, desired to keep the paddle, which was an old one but good enough as a curiosity, and he would willingly have paid a higher price for it at the outset, had it been asked. But now, as he remarked to the boys, it did not seem advisable either to return it or to compensate the native further, for, if every transaction was to be re-opened at the whim of one of the parties, trading was not likely to be done on a very enduring basis, and no one could be sure when a bargain had been completed. So he gave the two to understand that the matter must rest as it was.

The Viola's people, having access now to their trading material, were as quick as the boys to begin exchanges on shore. One member of the expedition exhibited a serviceable kayak for which he had given two alarm-clocks and a quantity of colored beads and ribbons. Many were the implements of hunting and articles of apparel that were brought aboard and deposited in the staterooms that day, and everybody had interesting tales to tell.

Dinner was served by the Viola's French cook, and Caesar found himself out of a job. He could not be induced to go ashore, saying it could do him "no good ter git in de clutches ob dem savages," and there was almost nothing for him to do except to care for the belongings of his own party and keep their firearms in order. But he, as well as the others, needed a respite.

After dinner the four lads, to whom a change of activity was as good as a rest, set off to climb the heights back of the village. As they passed through the native quarter they saw a woman carrying spring-water in a little cask on her back, and though her burden was heavy she willingly stood for her picture. She walked as all the Eskimo women do, with a bent, slouching gait.

As they proceeded, the boys saw fish drying upon

poles, and in some places open-air cooking was in progress over fires of roots. Phil stopped several times to photograph these domestic scenes.

From the far side of the settlement a faint path led through a grassy, spongy meadow, and was lost among the rocks where the cliffs began. There were clefts in these precipices by which the four could ascend. Reaching the top of the crags, they clambered on over a barren, broken surface of granite. There was very little soil to be seen, the ice-sheet of some former period having swept it away and scoured the hilltops into their present rounded contours. Often the easiest path lay over the remains of some old snowdrift that levelled the rough bed of a ravine. In places the surface of this old snow was tinted a beautiful pink. Ralph hailed this as the " red snow " of Arctic writers, and declared that it was caused by a minute vegetable growth. He did not venture, however, to collect any of it in his tin case.

In one of the mountain gorges two or three boulders were found suspended between the walls like the famous rock which formerly hung in the Flume in the White Mountains of New Hampshire. And here, also, Malcolm came upon a blue mussel-shell, doubtless brought from the shore by a sea-bird.

In the deeper hollows were lakelets and marshes, the latter retaining a shallow soil which supported green turf and a few modest flowering plants. Of these Ralph carefully collected specimens for future study.

Arriving at the highest level, it was clear that they stood upon a large island, — a fact they had hardly appreciated hitherto. A strait a few miles wide, dotted with smoothly polished rocky islets, separated them from the mainland, where snow-ribbed, purple mountain peaks were visible. Here and there between them glistened, like a white wall, the inland ice, — that enormous glacier which covers all Greenland except occasional strips of coast, none of which much exceed a hundred miles in width. Malcolm explained that it is from this inland ice where it reaches the sea or some deep fiord that the largest icebergs are launched, and his companions now recalled with new interest the thrilling narratives of Nansen, who crossed it at the south from east to west in 1888, and of Peary, who crossed and returned over the northwestern part in 1892.

After clambering up and down almost inaccessible cliffs, the boys seated themselves to rest and to watch an interesting phenomenon on a prominent peak called Igdlerfik, or, in the Danish, Kistefjeld, 2930 feet high, situated across the strait. A damp

" Here and there glistened the inland ice." (*Page* 144.)

wind was blowing in from the sea, and the cold summit of the mountain condensed the moisture while it was yet several hundred feet away. The result was the formation of a cloud which wreathed the cone continuously. The strong wind was all the while blowing this cloud past the mountain and inland in trailing shreds of mist, but at a distance of half a mile or so these were totally dissolved again. In the very teeth of the gale the denser part of the cloud feigned repose, being renewed on the one hand as fast as it was torn away on the other.

Upon returning to the ship the boys found that a large party of the Viola's people had come in from the glaciers, thirty miles away in Isortok Fiord. Kayakers had been sent out for all the others, as Professor Roth hoped to continue the voyage northward with little delay.

That evening the Eskimos gave a dance near the flagstaff on a sanded bit of level ground, and several of the sailors participated. Two native fiddlers furnished good music. There were two kinds of dances, — one a sort of waltz, and the other something like the lanciers. In the latter, upon the recurrence of certain strains in the music, the dancers stamped three times, clapped hands three times, and then shook their index fingers playfully in their partners' faces, all the while keeping time with their feet. They were very merry and seemed eager to dance as long as the slowly fading twilight lasted.

CHAPTER XII

KAYAK, OOMIAK, AND LIFEBOAT

WHEN the boys went on deck the following morning Professor Roth called their attention to some Eskimos hovering near the steamer in their kayaks.

"A Greenlander afloat in his kayak," said the Professor, "becomes as much a part of it as the Indian is of the pony he rides. His control of it is absolute. He can skim swiftly over calm waters, or balance unerringly in a heavy sea. The little craft answers the lightest touch of the paddle. Watch, now, — those fellows are going to show us some tricks."

As he spoke, one of the kayakers was seen to apparently lose his balance, in spite of boasted skill. The kayak rolled over, and the occupant disappeared under water.

Andy shrugged his shoulders. "Ugh!" said he. "That's nothing new. I did that myself, yesterday."

This brought a laugh from Malcolm and Ralph and Phil, who retained a vivid recollection of his adventure. But they kept their eyes on the kayaker, or rather on the bottom of his canoe, to see what would happen.

Slowly the overturned craft was seen to be completing the circle, and in another moment a skilful twist of the paddle brought the man up on the side opposite to that on which he went down. He had retained his paddle and his place through the whole performance, and now sat grinning at the spectators on the steamer. They applauded heartily.

" He must have got soaked," said Phil.

" Oh, no," replied the Professor. " You see he is wearing a seal-hide jacket and hood in one piece. His sleeves are bound tightly to his wrists, and the jacket fits snugly over the raised rim of the cockpit. He's probably a little damp around the edges, but by no means wet through. And you see the kayak rides as buoyant as ever."

Another favorite performance was now executed by two kayakers. The first stationed himself at right angles to the second, and held his paddle across the kayak in front of his body to keep it out of the way. Then the second retreated a little to gain a good impetus, and shot his kayak straight at the other, aiming just behind its occupant. The result was not a collision, as might have been expected, for the over-reaching prow of the advancing canoe mounted the stationary craft as a sleigh-runner takes a ridge of snow, bore it down somewhat, and then rode over the tough seal-hide without giving or receiving any injury.

" Even the little boys are expert in the use of the kayak," observed the Professor. " Their training begins at the age of six or eight. They have a game which imitates the more serious occupation of their fathers, and you may see them at it to-day if you watch. Five or six of them embark in their diminutive kayaks, taking along their toy bird-darts and walrus-spears. The dart consists of a shaft of wood about four feet long, tipped with a point of bone. Some distance back from the point three notched and barbed pieces of bone flare out from the shaft to entangle the bird if the point misses. The spear is similar, but it is longer, and has no bone attachments midway of the shaft.

" Having reached a spot where the water is calm and there is plenty of room, one of the boys holds his paddle straight up above his head. The others, one by one, throw their darts and spears from a distance of twenty or thirty feet and try to strike the paddle. By frequently playing this game they become quite skilful and are able to use their bird-darts to good advantage against ducks and gulls. But there is always some danger to the boy who holds the paddle. One little fellow with his cheek gashed by an ill-aimed spear was brought to one of our physicians for treatment a few days ago by his mother. He submitted like a Spartan while the doctor washed and sewed up the wound.

" You 'll find it interesting also to notice the kayakers when they start out equipped for seal hunting. Each carries on the deck of the kayak, immediately in front of him, a framework something like a three-legged stool, the round top of which is encircled by a rim about two inches high. Within this rim is coiled a long line, one end being attached to the spear. Behind the hunter rests an inflated sealskin. When a seal or walrus is speared, this sealskin attached to the other end of the line can be thrown overboard to float upon the surface and mark the position of the animal. It also tends to prevent the body from sinking. Usually the hunter's food on these expeditions is a great chunk of raw blubber carried on the deck in front of the framework, and washed now and then by the waves that splash over the prow."

The boys thought this would prove rather rough

fare, but they refrained from comment, seeing that the Professor had more to tell them.

"When a seal or any kind of game is brought to the settlement," continued their friend, "all the work of skinning and cutting up the animal falls to the women. The sole duty of the men is to procure the game. That done, whether with little labor or much, they have nothing further to do until their captures have been transformed by the industry of the wives and mothers into food, and oil, and clothing, and hides for the covering of kayaks. The preparation of the hides for almost any use is a matter of no little toil. The women must chew their edges to make them pliable enough to be sewn into boots or boat-coverings, and as a result the teeth of every woman beyond middle age are worn down nearly to the gums. When one considers the exceeding toughness of seal-hide, the incredible labor of this task may be imagined."

The breakfast call now sounded, and the Professor and his hearers adjourned to the dining-saloon.

Soon after breakfast one of the ship's boats was made ready for a journey which the Professor had planned. Two of the passengers were to accompany him, together with Zuckbias, the chief Eskimo, and one of his men. The four lads eagerly accepted an invitation to be of the party. It was the intention to visit ancient burial-places in search of native skulls, which were desired by a museum for comparison with those of other races. They passed around to the east side of the island, where, in a little cove that was noticeable for its sandy beach, they landed and found themselves at Sukkertoppen's cemetery. In the hollow between two walls of rock that might have been fifty feet high and two hundred feet apart, with sides grooved and scratched by prehistoric glaciers, were perhaps fifty small wooden crosses, most of them whitewashed, marking the location of the later graves. Two or three plots were enclosed by neat picket fences and were doubtless Danish. The wood used in the cemetery was imported from Copenhagen, and it seemed remarkable that in a region so well supplied with stones there were no monuments of that material; but doubtless it appeared to the natives more fitting to raise above their dead what was to them a costlier, less commonplace memorial. Throughout the cemetery the grass grew fresh and green as if nourished by the dust of the departed, and little wild-flowers blossomed here more abundantly than elsewhere. Beyond the cove and the strait rose picturesquely the distant mountains of the mainland.

On a low mound at one side the guides pointed out an old grave, — so old that nobody knew anything about the persons buried there, — and without any compunction helped the white men to open it. First they removed some round rocks that were piled upon the top, then a few inches of soil, and there, hardly a foot deep, were several skeletons fairly well preserved. The skulls alone were taken, then soil and rocks were restored. A second burial-place, marked by stones piled under an overhanging ledge, was found to be so ancient that the bones crumbled and could not be saved. On the return a third spot was visited upon a rocky islet, and yielded four or five good skulls with the teeth intact.

That afternoon the boys made a novel voyage to the loomeries, or bird-rocks, beyond the Sugar Loaves. This excursion was taken in an oomiak, or woman's boat. Eskimo women never use the kayak, and, *vice versa*, the Eskimo men never embark in an oomiak except one steersman. The oomiak is very much larger and wider than the kayak, being often over thirty feet long and five feet across in the centre. It is constructed of seal-hides sewn together and stretched tightly over a frame of wood or bone. Not being decked over, it is adapted only to waters comparatively quiet, and is used for transporting families from place to place or for bringing home reindeer and other heavy game. The oars have wide but short blades, and are fastened to the gunwales by thongs of seal-leather.

Five women manned the oomiak, as one of the party expressed it. The steersman, with his paddle, took his place at the stern, and eight Americans, including Henry, Malcolm, Andy, Ralph, and Phil, disposed themselves as best they could. One heavy man almost punched a hole through the bottom of the craft when he stepped in, for he missed the wooden framework entirely and brought all his weight upon the seal-hide bottom. The tough skin stretched but did not split.

The crew ranged from wrinkled old age to the belle of the village, seventeen years old. This girl was comely of form and feature, with a clear olive complexion through which the red blood showed in her cheeks. She was very desirous to accompany the party, and having obtained permission at home she came running down to the waterside beaming with smiles and dressed in her very best, which included a bead necklace and immaculate white kamiks. Her name, phonetically spelled, was Galeepa Layput.

Each woman took a single oar, two rowing on one

An Oomiak, or woman's boat. (*Page* 154.)

The Viola. (See page 156.)

side and three on the other, and soon the oomiak moved gaily out of the harbor and along the coast inside a chain of small islands. The stroke rowed by the crew had several peculiarities. At first it was regular in time, but the women rose a little from their seats as they leaned forward, so that their whole weight came into the backward and downward pull. A little later they varied the time by two short strokes and a long one. When one of them wished to change the stroke or go more slowly she said "tahma," and the others never failed to heed.

Before reaching the loomeries several big Arctic gulls were shot, also some murres and a few young geese. Occasional stops were made to allow pictures to be taken, but after about two hours the oomiak came under the great cliffs where millions of birds were nesting. A gunshot here almost darkened the sky with the multitude of screaming fowl, and all along the ledges the young birds, too small to fly, were stretching their necks to see the cause of the commotion.

It was a long distance back to Sukkertoppen, and the crew, though very willing, had blistered their hands badly on the outward trip. The Americans therefore let them ride as passengers on the return and did the rowing themselves. Being thus relieved of all labor, the women were free to exercise their curiosity. Several of them essayed to smoke cigars, which one of the men offered in a spirit of fun, but for some reason they did not persevere after a few puffs. One and all were eager to try on the gloves of civilization and possess themselves of handkerchiefs, and finally each was made happy with a handkerchief. They were much astonished when allowed to look through a pair of field-glasses. One of the older women opened her mouth in amazement when she saw distant objects apparently draw near, and when the glasses were reversed she stretched out her arms to signify that everything had gone far away. It was quite beyond her comprehension.

Knowing that they had good voices, the Americans urged them to sing, and after much coaxing and presents of needles they rendered two or three little hymns very sweetly, and then stuck the needles in their topknots.

The evening was partly gone when the steamer was reached, but it was still broad daylight. Most of the passengers had gone ashore to take leave of the Danes, for it was planned to leave Sukkertoppen early in the morning. The officials and their families had been entertained on board the Viola during the absence of the party in the oomiak, and now

A visit to the steamer.   (*Page* 157.)

returned the compliment handsomely. The ladies sang and played upon the piano, and regaled their guests with the best the house afforded. The boys hurried through their supper and went ashore in time to participate in the festivities, though perhaps that is not quite the right word, since the sadness of a life-long parting was in it all. There could be little doubt that the hosts and their guests would never meet again.

The Eskimos now hovered about with many things to trade, and there was brisk bargaining. Most of them had already learned to say such words as " tobac," " money," " no good," " bimeby," " water," " nuff; " and the Viola's people had learned that " ap " meant " yes," " nahmee " meant " no," and " ahyungulok " was the equivalent for " all right," and they could call most of the implements of the chase and articles of dress by their native names. There was one bright-faced little Eskimo boy, with straight black hair cut off just above his eyes, who had learned the exclamation " Hello! " and used to repeat it as often as he saw a white man. He was soon known as Hello, and possibly is still called by that name.

When at last the passengers were leaving to go on board the steamer, the Eskimos gathered in front of the Inspector's house and sang a farewell song in the dim light. These simple souls were so good-hearted and friendly that they needed no suggestion, but came together spontaneously, as it seemed, to bid good-by in this way. Clear and sweet their voices sounded in the stillness of that solitude, and more than one heart was touched, not only by the intrinsic sweetness of the song, but also by the perfect childlike grace of the act.

CHAPTER XIII

A SUNKEN ROCK

SOME time during the night the last stragglers returned from the glaciers of Isortok Fiord. When the boys awoke, the throb of the machinery told them that the steamer was in motion, and a glance through the ports showed the green waves rolling past. Hastily dressing, Phil went on deck at about seven o'clock, leaving Malcolm to take another nap. The harbor was not far astern, and the steamer was proceeding slowly and cautiously under the guidance of a native pilot, for rocky islands and half-hidden reefs were visible in various directions. Captain Ayre, Henry, Andy, Ralph, and Caesar, were all on deck before him, and Phil joined the group.

"Are we off for the North Pole?" he asked.

"There or thereabout," answered Andy. "This beats stoking all hollow, does n't it?"

"Yes," said Phil. "I should n't want to be down in that hole when the ship is rolling like this."

The sea was in fact quite rough, and there was wind and rain in plenty, yet a large number of kayakers had accompanied the Viola thus far, balancing from wave to wave with marvellous dexterity. But, when a mile out, they left, pilot and all.

Threatening as was the weather, it had been decided to put to sea and head north for Disco Island, for already it was the ninth of August, and the Arctic summer is brief.

Soon the watchers went below for breakfast, then Phil returned to the stateroom, where he busied himself in folding up and packing away his camera, which had been left fastened upon its tripod. Malcolm was still in his bunk, but roused himself a little as Phil entered.

"What's the time, old man?" he inquired sleepily.

"About half-past eight," said Phil. "Are n't you going to get up?"

"Not just yet. I don't feel first-rate. Late suppers don't agree with me."

It was unusual for Malcolm to be under the weather, and Phil was about to question him further when a faint, almost imperceptible tremor passed through the ship. Malcolm realized the cause instantly, and his face blanched as he looked quickly out through the port. They were going at full speed now.

"Phil," he cried, "did you feel that? It was a — "

Before he could end the sentence there was a terrible jarring bump that nearly threw Phil down. In the dining-saloon dishes went crashing off the tables, lamps fell from their sockets, and there was pandemonium in earnest. Following the bump the steamer careened to starboard and ripped along upon her side with a horrible sound of rending iron. Malcolm, in spite of his recent resolution, came out of his berth with one bound, while Phil clutched at the side of the doorway for support. Then the ship rose upon a wave and righted, but only for a moment. Sinking into the trough again she crashed once more upon the hidden reef. Again she rose, and for the third time she pounded. Was she going to be impaled, or would she go over into deeper water? The lads had no idea, and indeed they hardly knew which was to be preferred. But after the third shock there came no others. The steamer's headway, now almost wholly lost, had been barely sufficient to carry her across.

As soon as they could keep their feet the two rushed out to the companionway, jumping over broken crockery and all sorts of débris, to join the excited throng of men who were hastening toward the deck. A single impulse possessed all, — to get up into the open air, where they would have at least a fighting chance for life. The thought of being caught below like rats in a trap was not pleasant. Some of the passengers were dressed, others not. Some had grabbed up a satchel or a coat, and some had abandoned everything. Some were shouting for order, others pushing and crowding. As for Phil, he retained a dim recollection of having his jack-knife open in his hand at the moment when they struck, and of thinking he might as well drop it anywhere since all was lost. He did not remember shutting it up and replacing it in the usual pocket, but there it afterward proved to be. Nobody dreamed that the ship could float more than a few minutes, and every face turned shoreward as the deck was reached. The rain had ceased and the land was visible, but oh, how far away it seemed! Seven miles at the least, — seven miles of rough and ice-cold waters intervening. Yonder, astern and a little to the north, a reef ran out toward the ship, but there was no sign of a rock at the point where she had pounded.

On the bridge stood Captain Barrett calmly giving

orders and conferring with Professor Roth. Captain Ayre went also to the bridge to offer his services. Presently that baleful sound, the hoarse whistle of a steamer in distress, vibrated across the stormy sea again and again. Mr. Dahl, the second mate, brought powder, and loaded and fired the brass cannon on the upper deck in the hope that boats would be sent out from Sukkertoppen. Meanwhile the engineers and the carpenter had been ordered below to ascertain the situation. While awaiting their verdict, those who were not dressed returned for their clothing, but all were soon on deck again. Henry rounded up Caesar and the boys amidships and cautioned them to keep together and be ready for orders. To the surprise of all, the engineers and carpenter, after a hasty tour through the hold, reported that they could find no water coming in. The Viola was then headed shoreward cautiously at slow speed.

A few minutes later there was a fresh alarm. Information came that water was entering the stokehold and that the firemen, who up to this time had behaved well, were deserting their posts. Full speed was accordingly rung for at once, regardless of rocks and reefs. It began to look as if Henry and his little band of campers might have to go down into

the fire-room again and take the places of the igno-
rant and panic-stricken men, whose work they had
so thoroughly learned to do. The boys, with anxious
but determined faces, stripped off their coats and
made ready. But the alarm proved to be false, the
stokers were reassured and ordered back, and speed
was reduced again.

It was noticeable, however, that the steamer had
settled lower in the water than she should be, and
this could only be explained by the supposition that
there was an extensive leak somewhere that must
soon end the Viola's career. It was thought best to
send a boat ashore for assistance, as none was in
sight, and Henry's party, all of whom could row,
were detailed for this duty and requested to stand
aft by the starboard lifeboat ready to launch her.
Since the steamer was all this while coming nearer
to the land at a faster rate than they could row,
they were to wait for explicit orders before lowering away the lifeboat, but the stanch little craft
was swung out from the davits and provided with
extra oars.

As the moments dragged by with the steamer still
afloat, confidence in her safety began to increase.
One of the scientists went into the forward hold and
resumed the skinning of birds. The crew and the

cooks disappeared to their respective quarters, and the wreckage in the dining-cabin was cleaned up.

At last two kayaks were sighted battling with the big waves. They arrived an hour and a half after the accident. Zuckbias, the Eskimo chief, was in the first, and one of his men followed closely. These noble fellows had strained every nerve to make good time against both wind and sea, and when they had made their kayaks secure and climbed to the deck they fairly staggered. Almost before they had regained their breath they cried, "No good! No good!" and made frantic signs to go astern. The Viola had been heading, it appeared, directly for other hidden dangers, and now Captain Barrett was only too glad to follow the guidance of these faithful men. Not till they had seen the ship headed safely toward the deeper channel did they think of themselves and ask for the water for which they were thirsting. By the time they were somewhat refreshed the Inspector's white whaleboat was sighted. She brought Petersen, the best pilot in the settlement, and before long the Viola was back in the harbor with a very thankful crowd of men on board.

A more thorough examination of the vessel was now made, and the water-ballast tank under the engine-room and stoke-hold, which had been empty, was found to be filled with water which the pumps could not clear. This tank was about four feet high in its highest part, and its width was the width of the ship. The iron skin of the ship, forming the bottom of the tank, was evidently cracked and torn, but the injured plates were completely out of reach. Two small leaks forward of the tank were located and stopped by the engineers. The top of the tank was now virtually the bottom of the steamer and was all that prevented her from filling and sinking. Nobody knew how long its thin and rusted iron could stand the unwonted pressure. But one thing was clear, — the Viola was unfit for further voyaging.

Inspector Bistrup having returned from God-thaab, Captain Barrett, Captain Ayre, and Professor Roth went ashore to confer with him and Assistant-Inspector Baumann. The Inspector said he had supposed the whistling due to sighting some other vessel, but when he heard the gun he remembered the rock which a Danish steamer had encountered some years before. The chart in the Viola's pilot-house did not show this rock, but one of the passengers had a map on a larger scale which marked it with a little round dot. Small as it was, it had been found unerringly. Its depth must have been full three fathoms, and in a calm sea the ship would never have touched it.

The conference of officials resulted in the announcement that the steamer would remain at Sukkertoppen a week or more. Six American fishing schooners were reported to be cruising for halibut off Holsteinborg a hundred miles north, and from them alone could assistance be expected. The Falcon, Peary's relief steamer, would be returning from Melville Bay before long, but she was far too small to accommodate so large a party, and it was doubtful whether she could be intercepted.

As soon as it became known that Sukkertoppen would be their headquarters for a considerable period two parties were formed, — one intending to explore the Similik glacier, the other to hunt reindeer around Isortok Fiord. Their numbers, of necessity limited, were fully recruited before the boys learned what was going on, and it was with great disappointment that the latter found themselves compelled to stay aboard the Viola. It sometimes happens, however, that the last become the first. Henry had a plan in mind which he thought would interest them, and he sent Ralph and Phil to summon all the members of their party to his stateroom. Andy and Malcolm quickly arrived, eager to know what was doing, and

Captain Ayre and Caesar, followed by the two mes-
sengers, came shortly after. They all found seats
on the sofa and lower bunk.

"To begin with," said Henry, taking his stand
in the open door, " I shall assume that all or most
of us would prefer a chance to see more of Greenland to a week or more of inactivity here. There
appeared to be no chance for us to accompany either
the scientific or the hunting party, for, as it was,
they needed all the Viola's boats. We shall therefore have to look in another direction. Now I
understand that a relief party will have to attempt to reach one of the American schooners,
and I've been thinking that if Professor Roth
will accept our services we might volunteer for
that journey."

A shout of approbation greeted this speech, Captain Ayre and Caesar alone remaining unmoved.
The Captain expressed himself as heartily in favor
of the idea, but he could not tell whether he himself
might not be needed on the Viola. He was quite
ready to leave that question to Professor Roth and
Captain Barrett. Caesar, when pressed for his
opinion, declared his firm conviction that Phil and
himself would do well to remain on the steamer.
"Ebery time I see dem savages," said he, "I git

creepy feelin's in my spine. I ain' jes' ready fo' ter be scalped yet awhile, an' I don' b'lieve Phil am."

In view of the extreme mildness and unfailing good-nature of the Eskimos, it was hard to account for Caesar's notion. However, no amount of argument availed to dispel it

The majority being clearly in favor of Henry's proposal, Andy was sent to invite Professor Roth to the stateroom. Upon his arrival Henry tendered the services of the party for the relief expedition.

The Professor's face lighted up instantly. "You've certainly helped me out of a dilemma, Mr. Hollister," said he. "Nearly all my younger men have gone, and the crew would all be needed here in an emergency. But I am, as you say, under the necessity of organizing a party to go to Holsteinborg, and I accept your offer with hearty thanks, though after what you have already done for us it seems like imposing on you."

"No, Professor," said Henry, "we ask it as a favor. How many of us do you need?"

"Five, I should say. We shall have the Inspector's whaleboat and an Eskimo crew, and we must leave room for provisions and equipment. Five will be enough."

" Out you go, Caesar," said Phil, merrily. " You can have your wish and stay on the Viola."

" Bress de Lawd! " exclaimed Caesar. " An' yo' too, Phil. Dey ain' got no room fer yo' nudder."

" Oh, that 's another matter," said Phil, suddenly sobering. " I hope they have. Are you going, Captain ? "

" I would suggest," put in the Professor, " that Captain Ayre remain to assist Captain Barrett. The steamer 's in bad shape, and his advice may be wanted."

" Very well," said the Captain.

Ralph hereupon slapped Phil on the back and told him that if he would promise to behave he might go. But the Professor's face grew serious.

" This journey is no light matter, my lads," said he. " Don't enter upon it too thoughtlessly. First weigh the situation carefully, and then if you wish to take the chances with me, why, all right. This will be a voyage of a hundred and forty miles as we shall have to go. It will have to be made in an open boat, and there will be discomfort and hard-ship — perhaps perils — which we cannot entirely foresee. It is, however, a necessary undertaking, for without a convoy to the Viola we could not safely attempt to get home. We should be obliged in that case to stay here all winter, which would mean not only serious inconvenience and loss to our collegians and business men and six months of worry to our friends at home, but also quite probably a scarcity of food and a good deal of suffering. We should have to distribute our passengers and crew along the coast, a few in each settlement, and all in comparative discomfort. So the relief expedition must be undertaken by some of us; but I want no one to go who has not considered carefully and chosen deliberately. We shall make our preparations at once and start after supper to-morrow."

Needless to say, none of the five had any more desire to withdraw after the Professor's remarks than before. If anything, they were the more enthusiastic for the undertaking.

CHAPTER XIV

NORTHWARD IN AN OPEN BOAT

TOWARD five o'clock of the tenth of August the Inspector's boat came alongside. She was about twenty-five feet long and entirely open except a few feet of deck at the stern. She was sharpie-rigged, but the two slender masts could be unstepped almost instantly and the craft converted thus into a large rowboat. One-eyed Jacob Neilson was to be pilot and steersman. Three Eskimos were to manage the sails, row, and make themselves generally useful, while a fourth was to accompany the boat in his kayak as messenger and retriever of game-birds.

Provisions for about ten days were placed in the whaleboat, together with guns, ammunition, cameras, sleeping-bags, oilskin suits, and two tents. Thus equipped, the relief party set sail with cheers and Godspeeds from the Viola's deck ringing in their ears, and in their hearts a strong determination not to return without succor.

It was Jacob's intention to follow the passage inside the chain of small islands which lie along the west side of Greenland, for though this course would add about forty miles to the voyage it would insure comparatively calm waters. At the last moment Caesar had brought out Phil's belt and hunting-knife and insisted that he should gird himself with these for defence against the natives. The sky was still overcast, and a fickle, gusty wind was blowing. No sooner were they fairly out of the harbor than the waves began to splash into the boat, and occasional bailing had to be done to keep the provisions dry.

"Better put on the oilskins now, boys," said Henry.

Accordingly these were donned at once, and they kept off the chill as well as the spray. But soon, in the lee of the first small island, there was smoother sailing. The rugged Sugar Loaves being left astern, other and higher mountains on the large island of Sermersut and on the mainland rose prominently ahead, their summits capped with clouds and their rocky sides streaked with snow. Just as the dusk was deepening, the boat skirted the base of one of these peaks, whose majestic slopes came quite to the water's edge.

As the evening advanced, the wind became so strong and squally that the mainsail was lowered and its mast unstepped. Fortunately the course lay for the most part in narrow, sheltered channels; but wherever to windward a ravine between the mountains or a break in the islands gave the squalls a chance, even the small triangular foresail was more than could be carried.

" We 're beating the kayaker," observed Phil, after several miles of this scudding. " He 's fallen way behind."

" Sure enough," said Henry, looking around. " He 's paddling at a terrific pace, too. He can't keep that up much longer."

Old Jacob gave no sign that he had taken notice of the kayaker's plight until long after the latter had been lost to sight entirely. Then at last he brought the boat to the shore at a grassy place near the remains of some old huts, and the whole party disembarked upon the greensward, glad of the opportunity to stretch their cramped limbs. When the kayaker arrived, both he and his craft were taken on board the already heavily laden boat, and they proceeded.

Soon it became necessary to cross the mouth of a deep fiord, and here the white-capped waters were at the full mercy of the blasts. One of the Eskimos held the taut sheet in his hands ready to let it go instantly, while the others crouched on the starboard gunwale and kept their keen eyes fixed on the waves to windward. They could locate the coming gusts by the unusual ruffling of the water, and at the warning cry, sometimes given by one, more frequently by the three together, their companion would drop the sheet like a flash. Even with the sail flapping and whipping harmlessly to leeward, the boat would careen with the force of the puff till the water came in and she was on the point of capsizing, while the occupants instinctively threw their weight against the wind as much as possible. The danger past, the Huskie would gather in the sheet again, and on they would scud as before, leaving a wake of foam.

Malcolm could not conceal his admiration for the seamanship of these natives, and more than once he broke out in exclamations of praise. " They 're simply perfect! " he declared. " They can read the water like a book."

The scene as they crossed that fiord is indelibly impressed on the memory of the six Americans. The little boat seems swallowed up in a great solitude. There sits old Jacob perched upon the stern, silent, grizzled, his one eye equal to any other man's two, his face impassive, picking out the course. His hands grasp the tiller-ropes, and his whole attitude is that of an old sea-dog. At his feet, crowded into a semicircle, are the Professor and Henry and the four youths muffled in their yellow oilskins, alert, but silent too, taking in all the weirdness and wildness of this strange experience, and hardly moving except to bail. Just forward of the group are heaped the provisions and equipment. The kayak rests along the starboard side and intercepts some of the spray. Near the bow the four watchful natives are tending the sail or mingling their guttural cries of warning with the rush of wind and sea. To starboard in the dim light stretches the storm-tossed fiord bounded by dark purple mountains, while in the opposite direction lie islands whose shores and reefs twinkle ever and anon with surf. Grandeur, and mystery, and beauty, and solitude — all are there.

Beyond the fiord they come into narrower waterways again. How old Jacob invariably finds the right channel is more than they can tell. He chooses unhesitatingly between a dozen openings. He seems to know the look of every island by night as well as by day, though there is neither buoy nor beacon to guide him. Thus they pursue their intricate course hour after hour, turning now this way and now that. The light does not wholly fail. Even at midnight there is a ghostly radiance not unlike clear moonlight, although the sky is clouded. Sometimes they can see reefs and shoals very plainly as they pass over them; and once, when there seems to be hardly a foot of water beneath the keel, Malcolm looks at Jacob inquiringly. But that individual sits immovable, gazing calmly forward; and as the water quickly deepens, the young sailor concludes that the old Dane has navigated here before.

But suddenly there is a slight bump at the stern, and for the first time something is wrong with Jacob. Doubtless he has never brought so heavily laden a boat into these waters, and has miscalculated her draught by an inch or two. It would be a more serious reflection on his skill to intimate that he has mistaken the depth of water. However it be, the whaleboat has struck bottom, or at least her rudder has, and it hangs unshipped and useless. The pilot, too, appears to have become helpless, as if he and the rudder were one piece of mechanism. He is not at all the calm, confident man of a few moments ago. The Americans do not understand the jargon he shouts to the Huskies, but the latter do, for they loose the sheet and get out the oars in quick time.

The wind is blowing them upon the lee shore not a hundred feet away. Just what old Jacob intends, Malcolm does not know; but seeing that he makes no move to slip the pins of the rudder back into their sockets, he concludes to do it for him. Crawling out on the narrow after-deck and lying down, he can dimly see through the clear water, and after a few unsuccessful attempts the rudder is restored to duty. Malcolm then shouts to Jacob, and he to the Huskies. The oars are drawn in, the sheet resumed, and they glide back into mid-channel.

"I wonder if we can't talk with the natives," said Henry, after a time. "On board the Viola I jotted down some of their words out of an old book of Arctic travels, and I believe it would be a good chance to use them."

"I should be interested to see the experiment tried," remarked the Professor.

Henry accordingly shouted "kikertak," which is supposed to mean "island." The Eskimos in the bow looked at him questioningly and did not seem to understand.

"Perhaps that word is obsolete," said the Professor, "or maybe you did n't pronounce it right. Try another."

There was just sufficient light for Henry to read

his list. After consulting it a moment, and seeing that there was an unmistakable reef over against the nearest shore, he shouted " ikarlok." This word they recognized, and there was an instant chorus of " Ap, ap," as they pointed to the foaming shoal. Then he tried other words, and was usually comprehended, the Huskies doubtless making up their minds that he was a very learned linguist.

The Professor had some knowledge of Danish, and presently opened communication on a limited scale with Jacob. He also knew many of the Eskimo words, and altogether it was evident that they could talk with the crew when occasion demanded. When words failed, signs would probably suffice.

Soon after midnight they crossed the mouth of a second large fiord (Kangerdlugsuatsiak), the waves here being much more threatening in size than on the former occasion. This time, however, the boat was running before the wind instead of across it, and the seas, though looming large as they toppled up astern, lifted her easily and rarely came aboard. On the far side of this wide expanse they entered at length a quiet channel sheltered on each side by high rocks and bearing some resemblance to a canal. A movement among the Huskies now led them to suppose a settlement near; nor were they mistaken.

It was about half-past one in the morning, and the daylight was perceptibly increasing, when they saw at the head of the inlet on a high knoll several buildings. A dog howled as the boat drew up toward the landing-rock. Then others took up the cry, until there was a full chorus. A few sleepy natives next appeared, and were informed by the crew as to the identity and object of the party. The Professor learned upon inquiry that the village was Kangarmuit, otherwise called Old Sukkertoppen. The heavy boat had travelled about forty miles in eight hours with one little sail.

Quickly the tents were taken on shore, and preparations were being made to raise them on a grassy space near the boat when the chief trader gave directions that the Americans should make themselves at home in the loft of the church. This they were glad to do, and thither their sleeping-bags, oil-stoves, and some provisions were immediately transported, the crew being taken in charge for the rest of the night by their fellow Greenlanders.

The loft was a large one, and was used as a schoolroom, if one might believe the testimony of blackboards and maps and a few books. The sleeping-bags were placed on the bare board floor, and the six lost no time in crawling into them for such rest as they could get. It was soon discovered that a remarkable amount of cold air came up through the cracks of the floor from the church below, and even the Arctic sleeping-bags did not provide absolute comfort.

In spite of weariness, it was impossible for any of the party to rest later than nine o'clock, for the natives of the settlement were bubbling over with curiosity, and though they restrained themselves pretty well for a while, the impulse to catch a glimpse of the foreigners became at last too strong. They pushed the door open and crowded into and about the entrance, but with much less noise and loud talk than a similar crowd in America would have produced. So the would-be sleepers arose, and breakfast was soon preparing on the oil-stoves.

Ralph was the first to slip out of the loft and go down to the edge of the water to wash his face and hands. An Eskimo woman who was passing espied him, and paused at the top of the bank to see what strange performance this could be. She seemed utterly mystified by his ablutions, and apparently could see no sense in rubbing cold water over the skin, but she wished to know just how it was done. The brushing of the teeth was even more strange to her, and Ralph regretted for the moment that he was not as much of a magician as that passenger of the Viola who, on the way to the glaciers, had caused a stampede and almost a panic by taking his false teeth out of his mouth in the presence of a throng of natives. But Ralph's teeth happened not to be of that variety.

Breakfast consisted of pea soup, bread and butter, bacon, dried beef, smoked salmon bought from the natives, orange marmalade, crackers, dates, and cocoa. Andy and Malcolm tried a piece of seal meat, and reported that the flesh was fairly good but that they did not like the blubber. The others were quite content with looking at the raw red mass.

After breakfast the Danish trader invited the strangers to his house, where coffee was served. The trader's wife was an intelligent Eskimo, and they appeared to live in the utmost harmony and happiness. For the entertainment of the guests their son played upon the melodeon, and the new-comers were invited to follow, but there was no musician among them. Henry, however, rendered a few simple hymns, which seemed much appreciated.

It was learned here that the Swedish Government had sent out an expedition in search of the missing explorers, Bjorling and Kallstenius. These two men, accompanied by three Newfoundland sailors, had sailed from St. John's in June, 1892, with a very inadequate equipment for Arctic voyaging. Their vessel, the Ripple, was wrecked far north on one of the Cary Islands, and there one of the seamen died of disease. The others intended to escape in a whaleboat, as letters left in a cairn indicated, but from that time nothing further was known about them. It had been one of the purposes of the Viola's party to make a search of the coasts which they might have reached, but their own disaster had put this out of their power. The trader said that the American schooners were at the next town north.

The wind was now so strong and the clouds so threatening that it was decided not to resume the journey until better weather prevailed. There was ample time, therefore, for taking pictures of the village with its background of lofty and rugged peaks in the southeast across the fiord. The church was opened in order that its interior might be inspected and photographed, and here was found a font dated 1785 and inscribed with a text of Scripture.

There was also opportunity for trading, and in anticipation of that possibility the boys had brought along some articles which were in demand. The

Professor secured a curiosity in the shape of a large sail made entirely of dried seal-bladders sewn together. He also bought the skin of a gyrfalcon in good condition for mounting. Among the articles which were offered to the boys were the following, together with the goods they gave in exchange: two round bone trinkets for three needles, a basket for one needle, a toy kayak of wood for a negro doll, two scrapers of bone for a bandanna, a knife with wooden handle for a celluloid thimble and two needles, a salmon-spear with hooks for an American pocket-knife, a spear and bladder for a small saw, a file for a doll, a carved scraper of bone for a white handkerchief, a comb and scraper for a celluloid thimble, a sealskin purse for pieces of ribbon, a pipe of reindeer bone for a corncob, two stone arrowheads for a blue ribbon, a purse for a red ribbon, and five soapstone lamps shaped like shallow dishes for a bandanna or white handkerchief apiece.

In view of the chill wind the Professor had a regulation hooded blouse of cloth lined with downy birdskins made for him by the Eskimo women, who were able to turn out such clothing with wonderful celerity. He was also desirous of securing as curiosities several complete suits of Eskimo clothing for both sexes. Now it happened that the schoolmaster, a middle-aged man who might have been a half-breed, and who wore a full black beard as a mark of distinction, was sharp at bargains. On learning of the stranger's wish, and of his willingness to pay a grievously tempting price, the pedagogue sold him a pair of his wife's trousers, though he could not conceal his misgivings as to what would happen when she returned from a neighboring village.

"I'm sure he'll catch it," said the Professor, as he told the story and held up his prize for the admiration of his companions, "but I'm wondering *how*. There isn't a broomstick in the whole place."

CHAPTER XV

THE SOUTH STRÖM FIORD

WHILE the look of the sky was not reassuring next morning, it seemed best to delay no longer. The voyagers stepped into the boat at about ten o'clock, just as the schoolmaster was ringing the church-bell for the Sunday service. The meeting had to be postponed, however, for lack of a congregation, since all the people in the village were down at the shore to lend a helping hand and watch the embarkation.

The wind was fair and strong, but instead of clearing weather there soon came torrents of rain. Later, when the rain had ceased, the changing views of fiords and mountains were grand. A brief stop was made at a small settlement, but no new information about the schooners could be obtained.

During the whole day many wild-fowl flew about the boat. Great white Arctic gulls that measured several feet from tip to tip of their outstretched wings would soar above it, attracted by the novel sight of the sail. Sometimes their curiosity was ill rewarded, for it was necessary to replenish the larder. Phil happened to make two unlucky shots that looked easy, and each time old Jacob said " Ugh! " very much like an Indian. Had Caesar been present he would certainly have thought it a perfect imitation and quite sufficient proof that the old pilot had some of the blood of these " savages " in his veins.

One of the Eskimos now made signs that Phil should let him try. When the next gull came hovering over, the native brought it down unerringly. But Phil's fortune bettered presently, and the tone of Jacob's " Ugh! " changed accordingly. However, the boys had little relish for this shooting. The birds were so unconscious of danger, so innocently curious as they presented their beautiful snowy breasts to the guns, that no one had the heart to shoot them for mere sport; so, when the kayaker had picked up a full supply, the firing ceased.

It was better sport to shoot at guillemots, which now began to be numerous, for these duck-like birds, when resting on the water, would instantly dive at the flash of the gun and almost always escape, coming up in some other direction at a distance after two or three minutes. Only Andy had any success, and he killed but one. As yet no eider-ducks were seen, though a sharp lookout was maintained.

About the middle of the afternoon, as they glided out of a strait between an island and the main coast, there suddenly opened before them a magnificent panorama. They had reached the southern mouth of the South Ström Fiord, which divides the district of Sukkertoppen from that of Holsteinborg. The Professor, who seemed to know a good deal about the conformation of the coast, explained that this great fiord, a hundred miles or more in length, extending through the widest uncovered portion of the western side of Greenland from the ice-cap to the sea, is hardly navigable except at the turn of the tide, owing to its violent currents. Fortunately the hour was favorable, and, though the surface of the fiord was agitated and the waves decidedly choppy, old Jacob steered out upon it unhesitatingly.

Across this expanse and perhaps two miles away lay a large and mountainous island, which, to unaccustomed eyes, appeared to be the opposite mainland. After passing nearly over to the island shore the boat was headed east up the fiord, and now its occupants had the most impressive scenery that they were destined to see in Greenland. The southern

boundary of the fiord was a range of lofty mountains, their northern slopes a mingling of purple
rock and glistening ice and snow. The bases of
these mountains rose not infrequently in sheer precipices, and the glaciers of the peaks had flowed down
until they overhung the cliffs in dazzling frozen
waterfalls with silver streamlets pouring out beneath.
No wonder Jacob had preferred to sail along the
opposite shore, for sometimes, no doubt, enormous
masses broke away from these suspended glaciers.
Then woe to the boat that had ventured in too
close!

A few miles of this travelling brought them to
the eastern point of the island, where they turned
northwest down the smaller mouth of the fiord.
The sight of this waterway, as it opened out before
them, gave an overpowering sense of desolation and
loneliness. To the left, dark slopes heaped with
splintered rocks. On the right, mountains beyond
mountains far into the distance, with a weird,
unnatural light upon them, — the whole something
that Doré might have painted to illustrate the
"Inferno," or Bunyan imagined in the course of
"Pilgrim's Progress." The coloring and atmosphere of the scene suggested the uttermost part of
the earth, where no mortal eye had rested and no

human voice been heard. Indeed the spell of it was upon them all, and they sailed mile after mile in silence.

Toward six o'clock the boat was guided into a little cove where there was a beach of sand and gravel, and they all disembarked for supper. Hardly had they landed when Henry chanced to look back at the range of bold peaks across the main fiord. The next instant he was shouting, "Boys, look there!"

The others paused in their work and turned in the direction he indicated. As if to banish the feeling of gloom and desolation which had depressed them, gleamed high on the purple slope of a majestic mountain the glorious sign of the Cross. A vertical ravine intercepted by a shorter horizontal one, and both filled with pure white snow, accounted for the appearance, and the figure was as striking and perfect as that on the Mount of the Holy Cross in Colorado. Practical Phil, delighted, set up his camera immediately, leaving the others to wonder and admire.

It was possible to build a fire here, for there were many small dry twigs and sticks of driftwood along the beach, doubtless brought down on the waters of the fiord from the stunted thickets of willow and birch farther inland. While two or three of the lads gathered these, one of the Eskimos borrowed a shotgun and some cartridges and went to a near-by cliff where birds were nesting, whence he returned with a good number of gulls.

It was thought best to continue the voyage after supper, as the wind was favorable. The Professor became reminiscent, as they sailed along, of an earlier visit which he had made to Greenland, and the conversation turning upon the natives, he explained how they came by their numerous appellations.

" ' Innuit ' is the name by which they call themselves," said he. " That means ' the people.' "

" From their point of view, then, they would say, ' We are the people,' " remarked Henry.

" Exactly. The other races are outsiders, and probably came into existence by accident. These frozen regions are the center of the Universe to the Eskimos."

" And what becomes of Boston ? " inquired Ralph.

" Well, evidently Boston does n't occupy the hub, to their minds. It must be somewhere pretty well out on one of the spokes."

" I see," said Ralph.

" The term ' Esquimaux,' a French construction, or our word ' Eskimos,' signifies originally ' meat-

eaters,' but they do not like that appellation.
'Huskies' is a corruption of 'Eskimos,' and may
be attributed to the sailors, to whom is also due the
fact that the native word for a small child has come
to be 'pickaninny.' The natives are quick to learn
English words, but have some difficulty in combin-
ing them. For instance, when dredging the sea-
bottom for specimens one day, it seemed to an Eskimo
who was with us that the boat was moving too rapidly
for the best results. Thereupon he exclaimed, ' Small
quick plenty ketch 'em ! ' "

Late that evening a driving rainstorm set in, and
it grew dark and gloomy. The prospects for camping were most dismal, but about eleven o'clock, when
it was estimated that a day's journey of thirty-five
miles had been sailed, they landed on a marshy
island and made hurried preparations to set up the
tents, while two great ravens croaked like prophets
of evil over their heads. The muddy soil received
the tent-stakes readily, but that was the only com-
mendable thing about this spot. Every inch of
ground was sodden and spongy. Rubber blankets
had been brought, however, and these, spread within
the tent, kept the sleeping-bags dry, so that the travellers slept soundly and well.

It was still cloudy, with a fresh breeze, when day

dawned. They breakfasted on fried canned sausage, fried potatoes, bread and butter, crackers, dates, and cocoa, — not a bad repast for a desert island. A little later camp was broken, but they had proceeded only a mile when the wind increased so much and the clouds appeared so threatening that the weather-wise natives would go no farther. So the boat was turned toward a narrow inlet.

On one side of this inlet was a cave in the rocks large enough to hold several men. The Eskimos seemed to know this place and to have some reason for wishing to land there. Jacob steered inshore for them, and they immediately ran into the hole. The Americans could not imagine what was the object of their search until they heard a great flutter-ing and saw two half-grown eider-ducks come scam-pering out to the water. Luckily Phil had shells in his shot-gun, and he lost no time in making sure of these prizes, though it was such close range that the two fowls were not only plucked but also practically dressed for the kettle when he picked them up. All the other ducks in the cave were caught by the Eskimos.

CHAPTER XVI

AN ARCTIC HURRICANE

NOT far beyond the cave was a safe little bay, into which the boat was now brought and made fast to the rocks bow and stern. Meanwhile the wind was rising rapidly, and soon blew a tremendous gale from the southeast. With all haste a camping place was selected — the best that appeared — partially protected by a rocky ridge about twenty feet high that ran east and west. Had its direction been northeast and southwest the shelter it afforded would have been much better, but no other high land was anywhere in the immediate vicinity. The level ground north of the ridge was not so good for holding tent-stakes as that of the marshy island, and it was only here and there that a stake could be driven more than an inch or two without encountering a stone. Finally a few were driven deeply enough to hold temporarily, and the largest tent was then speedily raised. The Eskimos set their tent two hundred yards farther west, where the ridge curved to the southward. Thus they obtained better shelter, but had to camp on uneven ground and rocks.

Some of the provisions and dishes, the oil-stoves, guns, and sleeping-bags, were now transferred from boat to tent, and, as dashes of rain began to mingle with the spiteful gusts, the remainder of the cargo was covered with the sails and oilskins and made as snug as possible.

As they were returning to the tent after completing this work, the Professor paused to observe the signs of the sky.

"Look at those clouds, lads," he cried. "Do you see how the upper ones are seamed and rifted? Notice, too, almost overhead, those regular wavy folds. They are sure indications of strong winds. Now turn to the southeast and you'll see a lower stratum of flying scud torn into fragments by the shifting air-currents. It would n't take a weather prophet to read those signs. We are in for a big hurricane."

"No doubt of it," said Henry. "Look! There goes the tent!"

The canvas had collapsed and was now bellowing in the wind, which threatened to blow it into the bay. The Eskimos in one direction, and the Americans in the other, saw the danger at about the same moment, and all ran at the top of their speed toward the tent. Andy arrived first and gripped it hard.

"The stakes are all pulled up but one," cried he as the others came up.

"And that one is loosened," observed Ralph.

"We can't depend on the pegs, that's certain," said Henry. "We must collect a lot of big stones and lay them on the edges of the canvas. Bring up the heaviest ones you can find, fellows, while I drive the stakes again and get the tent into position."

The Professor and the Eskimos assisted Henry, and the tent was raised once more. Being then pinned to the ground by rocks of twenty or thirty pounds' weight on the south and east sides, it was likely to stand any gale that could blow, — or so its occupants believed, as they confidently took shelter beneath it.

But while they had been working, the storm had become even more furious. It was soon discovered that the tent-pegs were pulling out again, so the guy-ropes which could not be otherwise secured were made fast around large boulders, while an additional supply of rocks was piled upon the lower edges of the canvas. And now at last the little party felt justified in running in out of the blasts and making themselves as comfortable as circumstances permitted.

Within the tent it was by no means either calm or dry. The rain came almost horizontally, and struck the canvas with a sharp, crackling sound, like volleys of musketry. It not only struck, but came through. And with every gust the whole tent would squat down upon its inmates and sway and jump and tug and puff out and collapse till it seemed a living thing. Before long these gyrations caused many of the rocks to roll away from the edges. Then it was necessary to go out into a rain that stung the face like hail, and roll them back, and, if possible, reinforce them with more. But the boys rather enjoyed the excitement and novelty of battling with such powerful forces.

No sooner had the Eskimos put up their tent than they built a fire of moss in the lee of some high rocks and set their kettle on, preparatory to cooking their birds. Although they made no distinction between gulls and ducks, to a white man's palate there was a decided difference, the gulls having a strong fishy flavor. Hence the Professor went over and signified to Jacob that the ducks should be cooked for the Americans, and the Eskimos should retain the gulls. He carried with him such birds as he could collect, including the body of the guillemot, which Andy had skinned, and explained the case fully to the old pilot in Danish. The only bird which he did not take was one of the small eider-ducks, a part of whose plumage Ralph was planning to preserve.

At length, when it seemed that sufficient time had elapsed and the dinner had not arrived, Henry put on a rubber coat and went over to investigate. He approached the group around the fire just in season to see the last vestiges of the repast disappearing into the mouths of the Eskimos. They had eaten not only all the gulls, but also every duck, and there was nothing left but clean-picked bones and feathers. When Henry returned and reported, a hearty laugh went round at the expense of the Professor, who had to admit that the Danish language was not his strong point. But he promptly went to work and prepared a good meal on the oil-stoves.

After dinner the guns were thoroughly greased with butter, but there was no other work to do except to run out occasionally and examine the moorings of the tent. Malcolm, Ralph, and Phil lay down in their sleeping-bags for a nap, and Andy busied himself in bringing his diary up to date. By this time all had become accustomed to the antics of their canvas house, which ceased to disturb them save in unusual instances.

There was one such about the middle of the afternoon, when Phil, who had been soundly slumbering, sprang up in his sleeping-bag and began to thrash around wildly with his arms, while the Professor and Henry, who saw the expression on his face, roared with laughter. It turned out that one of the guy-ropes had loosened, allowing the wet canvas to sag against his cheek. He had been dreaming that he was back on the Viola, and at that cold touch he thought the steamer had gone down and he was struggling in the water. The two witnesses were so highly amused at the momentary panic depicted in the features of their usually imperturbable young comrade that it was some time before they could compose themselves.

Toward evening the wind abated somewhat, but strengthened again at midnight, and several times the two older men grasped the canvas, thinking the tent was about to be blown from over them. All the following day the gale continued with great violence. The rain even increased, and was dashed against the tent with such fury that everything inside was damp. Professor Roth and Ralph suffered a touch of indigestion which they attributed to the dates, and these were henceforth issued more sparingly. Ralph was also troubled with lumbago,

almost as effective as boiling water

finished, he and Phil went to take a
at, which lay a hundred yards or so
pool near the head of the little bay.
extraordinary amount of rain-water in
r five inches at the least — and while
been well protected from above, the
skins having been held in place by large
ne had thought of the possibility of so
in the bottom. With difficulty the two
far enough to clamber aboard, and ex-
goods. Some of the clothing was awash,
eral boxes of tinned provisions, but the
suffer no injury. What gave Phil much
n was the discovery that the wooden box
ll his photographic plates, both used and
an inch deep in the water. The card-
of a dozen plates each stood on edge in
box, hence he hoped that no more than
f the plates had been affected, but this
be known until they were developed.
e made haste to raise them to a safe
hen the condition of things was reported
Roth he set the Eskimos to bailing out

and kept his sleeping-bag all day — in fact for
thirty-six consecutive hours. It was not the best
sort of place for a hospital, but no complaints were
heard. To proceed even half a mile was out of the
question.

It was Andy's turn to get breakfast, and he bethought him of the one small duck which alone had
escaped the Eskimos' kettle. He boiled the bird,
and the soup was then divided into six equal portions and drunk out of tin cups. It was found to
have a very fine flavor. The meat was also divided, each getting about two mouthfuls. When
this was gone they had recourse to the regular
rations, though heartily wishing there were more
ducks.

Heretofore the Eskimos had washed all the dishes,
but as one of them had a constant cough and was
probably consumptive, while the habits of the natives
in general were not too cleanly, Andy took this task
upon himself, thinking he would rather run the risk
of being squeamish than the worse one of contracting
disease. Besides, he welcomed the chance to do something. He carried the plates, cups, knives, and forks
to a pool of sea-water formed by high tide in a cir-
cular hollow southeast of the tent. Here there was
plenty of sand and moss and seaweed, and the com-

bination proved almost as effective as boiling water and a dish-rag.

This work finished, he and Phil went to take a look at the boat, which lay a hundred yards or so north of the pool near the head of the little bay. There was an extraordinary amount of rain-water in her — four or five inches at the least — and while the cargo had been well protected from above, the sails and oilskins having been held in place by large stones, no one had thought of the possibility of so much water in the bottom. With difficulty the two drew her in far enough to clamber aboard, and examined the goods. Some of the clothing was awash, as were several boxes of tinned provisions, but the latter would suffer no injury. What gave Phil much more concern was the discovery that the wooden box containing all his photographic plates, both used and unused, was an inch deep in the water. The cardboard boxes of a dozen plates each stood on edge in this larger box, hence he hoped that no more than the edges of the plates had been affected, but this could not be known until they were developed. However, he made haste to raise them to a safe level, and when the condition of things was reported to Professor Roth he set the Eskimos to bailing out the craft.

That afternoon some extra food was cooked, but beyond that there was little to do. A few scraps of newspapers which happened to be in the tent were read and re-read with as much eagerness as if they had been messages from another world. And indeed the campers were cut off completely from all other living beings, stormbound in the midst of that great desolation.

The gale showed not the faintest signs of slackening yet, and once Henry and the boys made their way to the top of the ridge to see its full grandeur. It was almost impossible to stand on the exposed summit. One could lean with nearly the entire weight against that wind. They wondered that a cairn of loose stones which someone had piled there was not long ago blown over.

Prominent on the coastline to the southeast rose the dark mass of Mt. Kingatsiak, more or less obscured by clouds. Before them to the south and west was the open sea. Near at hand there was little surf, for it was an offshore hurricane, but the whole surface of the water was a froth of seething white foam and spray. Indeed the force of the blast was such that the waves seemed actually flattened by it, their tops being blown off and whirled away. Half a mile to the west lay several rocky islands, and these were white with a grand surf, the spray from which dashed clear over them. That the fishing schooners could ride out that gale in the open seemed incredible, but Malcolm was confident that they would do it if they had not succeeded in making a harbor.

Coming down from the ridge, Henry beat his way alone across the neck of land between the pool and the head of the bay to see what there was beyond, and presently came into a wilderness strewn with boulders. Wherever a little sand had lodged were fragile bluebells bending to the storm. But he did not go far. The wild gloom of the sky, the roar of the wind, the utter loneliness, wrought upon him — strong man that he was — as the dread of darkness upon the mind of a child, and soon he turned back to the fellowship within the tent.

At about eight o'clock in the evening Phil, who had been sleeping, awoke and began to busy himself around the stoves. Thinking he was intending to warm a bit of supper, the others, who had finished, gave no particular heed till he turned and asked, " What 'll you have for breakfast, Professor ? " The laughter which followed was the first intimation he had that it was not morning.

It was a little before midnight when the great storm ceased. As soon as this fact was discovered by the more wakeful ones the sleepers were routed out and a hasty meal was prepared, for it seemed advisable to continue the journey at once. Then the tents were taken down, the boat was bailed out again, and everything was put on board.

There was a wonderful charm about that early morning! It was growing toward full daylight at two o'clock when they embarked. The keen air was delicious with morning freshness. A colder temperature had followed the storm, and not only the mountains but also the lower hills about were sprinkled with new snow. Apart from the scenery, it was like a crisp November dawn in New England, with the mercury at about 35°.

The wind was fair though light, and after a sail of six or seven hours, with entrancing vistas of fiords and purple peaks and rugged isles, they came to the small settlement of Itivdlek, situated almost exactly upon the Arctic Circle. Ceremonies such as Father Neptune is wont to inflict upon the uninitiated on crossing the Equator might have been in order here, but the old sea-god did not put in an appearance. In fact, as the Professor remarked, he seems much less jealous of intrusion into his polar realm than he is in the case of his tropic one, and indeed has hardly been reported north of the Mediterranean.

Thoroughly chilled as they were by their long morning's ride, our voyagers were disposed to think his choice of a habitat a wise one.

Itivdlek was found to be a squalid and uninviting village. The people seemed both poor and unkempt, and the houses were mostly low huts of turf and stones. There was a great deal of offal and refuse lying about, and the smells were in keeping with the environment. Here, at the water level, there had been snow in the recent storm, and traces still remained in the shade of the houses, but in spite of the cold weather the whole place swarmed with voracious mosquitoes.

After the usual custom the local trader served coffee in his house. The new-comers were able to buy from him some rock sugar, the only kind he had, to eke out their failing supply. The price of their purchase was increased somewhat on account of the brown paper in which it was done up, that being evidently a luxury in Itivdlek, and not to be carried away gratis.

The Professor questioned the trader in Danish, and learned that an American schooner, whose skipper was Captain Lawson, had called there shortly before and would call again before leaving those waters. There were other schooners at or near Holsteinborg. The Professor accordingly wrote letters to be sent out by kayakers if any vessel were sighted. The party cooked a meal on the rocks, enduring the mosquitoes as best they might, while the forty or fifty Eskimos of the village watched them with great interest and scrambled for stray bits of bread and empty sardine cans.

It was nearly noon before they managed to get away from Itivdlek and the mosquitoes, with about thirty miles of voyaging still before them. About mid-afternoon they saw with anxiety that the wind was dying, and soon it became necessary to get out the oars. Fog settled down awhile, shutting out the distance as they rowed, but later it rose, enabling them to see on the shoulder of a mountain what looked like the broken columns and fallen ruins of an ancient city. It was hardly possible to believe that Nature, not Man, was responsible for these realistic effects.

At eight in the evening, after hard rowing, they turned a point of rock and suddenly found themselves in the fine harbor of Holsteinborg, five long days from Sukkertoppen. The natives had already seen them and were watching their approach from the heights, so the American flag was raised on the tip of the boat-hook and a salute of three shot-guns waked the echoes from cliff and crag. Three guns promptly answered from the town, and the Danish flag ran up to the peak of the flagstaff. Then three more guns from the boat, and the natives cheered. But pleased as they were to have reached their destination, the hopes of the relief party sank as they looked about them. Not a sail nor a mast was anywhere in sight. The harbor was empty.

CHAPTER XVII

HOLSTEINBORG

INSPECTOR MÜLLER was on the wharf to greet the voyagers as they disembarked. He was a thick-set man, with ruddy complexion and sandy beard. Born in the Faroe Islands, he spoke both English and Danish, and extended a cordial welcome. The Professor in a few words made known the members of his party and the object of their journey, and the Inspector at once invited them all to take supper at his house.

The village was built upon a hill overlooking the harbor. A smooth path bordered with luxuriant green grass led up toward it from the wharf. So vigorous was this grass that it seemed to the boys as if Holsteinborg must be south instead of north from Sukkertoppen. The party passed through a gate in a neat picket fence into the enclosure where the residence stood, a dark frame building with white window-casings, very much like Inspector Bistrup's house. At the northeast end of the enclosure were three or four storehouses of whitewashed stone. The native village appeared to lie in the other direction down along the slope of the hill.

Arriving at the house, the visitors were met by Frau Müller, a pleasant German lady. She spoke no English, and Professor Roth and Henry alone could converse with her. The Assistant-Inspector, Koch, his wife, and their little boy and girl, were also introduced, and later the missionary. These comprised the Danish colony at Holsteinborg.

It was a unique experience to come so suddenly out of a desolate wilderness into this civilized, home-like environment, and to sit down to a dining-table with snowy cloth, but the change was a very agreeable one. Frau Müller presided over the tea at one end of the table, her husband dispensed various viands opposite, while to wait upon the guests there was the most interesting servant they had ever seen — Louisa, an Eskimo girl about eighteen years old, with long red seal boots, bead necklace, red-ribbon topknot, and all the rest of the picturesque native costume. And what could have been neater for a serving-maid? Louisa was well trained, and attended strictly to her duties, as if she had been accustomed to seeing strangers all her life. In this respect she was an exception, the other natives taking

no pains to conceal their curiosity whenever the
foreigners were in sight.

Six hungry travellers were soon attacking the
good things with great relish. There was excellent
black bread and butter, accompanied by crisp round
crackers and cheese. There was pickled whale-skin,
soft and gray and about an inch thick, — a dish
new to the Americans. Smoked halibut and salmon
and potted meat completed the goodly bill-of-fare.

Four languages were in use around that table —
English, Danish, German, and Eskimo, — and such
a babel as there was withal! The guests brought to
their hosts the news of the wider world, and the
latter told about their life among the Greenland
natives. Owing to the monotony and isolation of
these Arctic posts, any inspector could retire on a
Government pension after serving ten years.

Inquiring as to the rights of vessels to fish off
the Greenland coast, the visitors learned that not
even the Danish vessels can legally do so. The
Inspector showed them the law, a copy of which is
given to every shipmaster entering a Greenland port.
This law is violated because there is no force to
compel respect of it. The inspectors are glad to see
the fishermen, and do not try to prevent their fishing,
or even their landing, if they behave themselves and

have no contagious disease on board. For the voyage of the Viola the Professor obtained a permit in advance.

The boys learned that, in addition to taking charge of the furs and ivory and oil which the Danish Government buys, and of the articles which are imported from that country, such as coffee, sugar, cloth, and wood, the inspectors act as judges in con-junction with councils of seven or eight of the chief natives. Criminal cases are very few. In Godthaab a man had pierced an oomiak and sunk it, drowning nine persons. He was brought to trial, but there was some doubt as to his criminal intent, and he received sentence of temporary imprisonment only. That had been the most serious case in a long time.

After an evening spent in devising plans for reaching one of the schooners, the Inspector led the way to a chamber in one of the storehouses, which was the only available sleeping-apartment in the settlement. The room was a large one, and contained a stove, chairs, and a big bed with eider-down mat-tress and pillows, and the whitest of coverlets. Hither the Eskimos of the crew, assisted by their friends from the town, had brought the provisions and equip-ment out of the boat.

" One thing is certain," observed the Professor,

as he looked the situation over, "that bed won't hold but two of us. We shall have to draw lots."

This was done, and the Professor and Phil were the lucky ones. The others spread their sleeping-bags on the boards of the floor and tried to forget the feathers.

Next morning Phil examined his photographic apparatus in the Inspector's dark-room, that official being himself an amateur photographer. On the voyage up the coast Phil had only been able to secure absolute darkness for changing the plates by crawling away down to the closed end of his sleeping-bag, where he was nearly stifled each time before the operation was accomplished. In the dark-room all was easy. The investigation showed that many of the plates had been dampened during the hurricane, but it seemed likely that they were not very seriously injured. He made no attempt to develop any of them here, not knowing at what moment the work might be interrupted.

The wood parts of the camera were so badly swollen by the dampness that it could hardly be opened for use in Holsteinborg. Phil managed, however, to take a few snap-shots, among which were two of the Inspector's team of Eskimo dogs. Twenty strong wolfish animals were harnessed to a heavy

sledge, and they dragged it over the dirt and grass
so vigorously that it was a wonder it was not wrecked
against some one of the buildings.

Soon after noon Professor Roth called Andy,
Ralph, and Phil, and asked them if they were ready
to climb a mountain in the interests of the relief
expedition. Ralph had heard Inspector Müller say
that he should have started on a reindeer hunt had
he not been prevented by their arrival, and he had a
vague hope that this was what the Professor had
in mind. It might be that a supply of reindeer
meat was even more necessary now than it had been
before. But this notion proved unfounded.

" What I want you to do," said the Professor,
" is to climb Mt. Praestefjeld, which, as you see,
forms the northern side of the harbor. It is two
or three thousand feet high. From its slopes or
summit you may be able to sight a schooner out at
sea, and in that case you are to report its distance
and position. One of the Holsteinborg Eskimos
will go with you to look after the boat. Are you
willing ? "

That the three were not only willing but eager to
go, it is unnecessary to state.

It was not a long row to the north side of the
harbor. As they came close in, a small blue fox

barked at them from the narrow beach of sand and then ran back inland.

" Botheration! " exclaimed Phil. " Why did n't I bring my gun? That pelt would have made a fine rug for my room at home."

But though they had brought along field-glasses and camera, their firearms, in the haste of departure, had been left behind.

It was evident before they landed that the conditions for an extensive view seaward were not improving. A steady rain had begun to fall, and the upper part of the mountain was now hidden by the clouds. But the lads started up the slopes nevertheless, taking what looked like the most feasible route. After scrambling up a bluff of gravel near the beach they came upon a plateau through a hollow of which ran a clear brook. All along the sides of this brook were thickets of willows not over four feet high and having the appearance of bushes rather than of trees, though doubtless this was as much of a forest as one would be likely to find in Greenland. Following the brook a quarter of a mile they discovered a beautiful waterfall, and at its base a pool whose banks were carpeted with the softest, greenest grass that one could wish to see. Phil was not content to proceed until he had taken the picture.

At this point they left the level ground and attacked the mountain proper, which here on the southeast side was less abrupt and broken than on that which faced the outer harbor and sea. But gradually they worked far enough around to the southwest to gain a wide outlook in that direction.

" There she is ! " exclaimed Andy, suddenly. " See ? Away down there toward Itivdlek ! A schooner with all sail set ! "

The glasses brought her out very distinctly in spite of the rain. " She's heading in toward the land," cried Phil, fairly dancing with joy and excitement.

Ralph thought she might be Captain Lawson's schooner, although another had called at Holsteinborg on the day before their arrival. The three took turns with the glasses until they had noted her rig and bearing. It was then agreed that Andy should return to Professor Roth at once with the news. Ralph and Phil, after pausing to look down on the village and across to lofty Mt. Kjerlingehaetten behind it, determined to push on.

Now they picked their way over rough rocks where tufts of stone-crop flourished, now crawled up smooth weather-worn ledges, and occasionally crossed swampy levels covered with green turf from which dandelions, asters, and other flowers were gathered by Ralph. The cloud-line was clearly discernible above, and just before they reached it the rain, to their surprise, turned to snow.

At the cloud-line Ralph balked.

"What's the use of going farther, Phil?" said he. "We can't see a thing if we get up into this fog, and my heart's beating like a trip-hammer."

"Oh, come on," panted Phil. "Let's go to the top anyway. I'm not going to stop here."

"But we're not in any kind of trim for climbing," Ralph objected. "That week in the boat and in the tent softened me all up. I'm thoroughly winded, and you're puffing like a steam-engine."

Phil admitted that he was. "All the same," said he, "I'm going clear to the top, even if I go alone."

So they had it pro and con for some minutes. Phil was at length persuaded to sit down with Ralph in the dryest spot that could be found to rest and reflect. Meanwhile Ralph brought forward his strongest arguments, but without success. His younger companion was bent upon conquering the mountain, irrespective of any other object. Ralph would not hear of his going alone, for if he should lose his way, or break a limb by a fall or misstep, it might go hard with him. So at last they started on together.

The two soon came to patches of old snow, which
grew more numerous and extensive as they ascended.
Then the climbing became harder, over slippery rocks
interspersed with snow. No longer was it possible
to see more than a few yards above or below, and
their only guide, apart from the slopes themselves,
was the sound of the waterfall which was still borne
up quite distinctly. They knew that if they kept
going up they must come to the top eventually, and
the waterfall assured them that they were on the
southeastern face of the mountain. At length they
came to a ridge with an abrupt declivity on the
northern side. Here the snowdrifts from the late
memorable storm were fully three feet deep. Following the ridge a short distance, they saw through
the thick air a cairn of stones marking the summit.
Against this cairn lay a long wooden pole, brought
apparently by some recent climber, though they
could not believe that any Eskimo would leave a
sizable piece of wood in such a place. Who had
preceded them here remained, therefore, a mystery.

It was snowing furiously on the summit, with a
high wind and a temperature of about 34°. The
two lads thought, as they stood there in a drift up
to their waists and a blizzard howling around them,
of their friends sweltering under an August sun far

away. But summer had left a trace even here. At the base of the cairn, where the wind had prevented deep drifting, Ralph found a yellow Arctic poppy bravely blooming in four inches of snow.

The boys paused only long enough to attempt a few photographs of themselves and the cairn in the midst of gray and white space, and then retraced their tracks, for they were very wet, and it would not do to linger in that wind. Below the snow-line progress was slower, since they had to pick their way cautiously down the ledges and listen once in a while to get the bearing of the waterfall. But as soon as they were out of the clouds it was a swift and easy journey down to the harbor, where, near the level moraine and beach, the Eskimo waited with the boat.

Later in the afternoon the rain in the village turned to big snowflakes, which fell thickly for an hour or two, but melted almost immediately. The air was so damp that Ralph and Phil despaired of drying their clothing. Their Danish friends would doubtless have dried the garments by the kitchen stove, but the boys did not like to make such a request. So, after putting on dry clothes, they hung the wet ones over chairs in the sleeping-room.

Soon afterward Phil was lucky enough to find an

Eskimo of about his own stature who was very desirous to own a cloth pair of trousers, and he offered him the pair which he had just discarded, in exchange for a seal-hide pair. The native looked the cloth trousers over thoroughly to all appearances, and did.not seem at all troubled by their damp condition, nor did he object to a small hole which Phil had worn or torn in the seat. With every evidence of satisfaction with the bargain he exclaimed, "Ap! ap! me speakum pants!" This was the equivalent of "Yes, yes, I will have my wife make you a pair."

He was as good as his word, and produced the new seal-hide trousers early next morning. An hour or two after the exchange had been made he returned to show the hole in the cloth pair, making signs to indicate that he had overlooked it in his previous inspection. As the Eskimos are sitting a great part of their time in their kayaks, the man had a real grievance in the location of this hole. It was where the rub came. Phil saw the point, and as he could not offer him a patch wherewith to mend the trousers he at least mended the wounded feelings of the native with a gift of a pocket-knife, and the Eskimo went on his way rejoicing.

Among the regulations of the Danish Government was one forbidding the use of kerosene in any of the

buildings.   Professor Roth had brought a can of it
for the oil-stoves, and this had been fetched from
the boat with the rest of the cargo.   The Inspector
chanced to notice this can and asked what it contained.   The Professor answered that it was oil,
and as Henry was engaged at the moment in cleaning his gun with it the Inspector's mind was eased
as to the character of the oil.   At least he said no
more about it.   But the Professor had no wish
either to mislead the Inspector or to violate any
rule.   The fact that the party were invited to take
all their meals at the Inspector's table made it unnecessary to burn the oil at all.

After their climb Ralph and Phil had the keenest of appetites, and the good Frau Müller antici-
pated their hunger.   She served for supper such
delicacies as tongue of reindeer, excellent scallops
from the harbor, and crisp radishes grown in the
little garden behind the house.   Her canary bird
sang as blithely as if he were in his tropic forest,
and in the window bloomed geraniums and other
flowers, so that the whole environment was home-
like and pleasant.

The Inspector informed his guests that an attempt
was being made to establish a colony for missionary
and trading purposes on the east coast of Green-

land. There were considerable numbers of natives in that region who were practically cut off from the rest of the world and obtained a precarious livelihood by hunting and fishing.

Henry took occasion to inquire whether the walrus was found in the waters around Holsteinborg, and was told that they were sometimes taken there, but not so frequently as farther north. It began to look as if the ivory they had hoped to secure would be as elusive as the furs.

Ralph remembered reading that the island of Ukivik, whereon were Norse ruins, and whose shores were said to be red with garnets, was near Holsteinborg, and he asked the Inspector if he knew the place. The latter replied that he did, but as the island was twenty miles away it might as well have been a thousand so far as the boys were concerned.

Professor Roth had sent out a kayaker in search of the schooner discovered from the mountain. After supper this man returned, saying he could not find her. But presently natives came to the house to announce that a dory was approaching. This was good news indeed, and all hastened out to see for themselves.

The little craft was already at the wharf, and soon up the path with swinging stride, clad in sou'westers and yellow oilskins and escorted by the entire Eskimo population, came five stalwart fishermen. It was a sight that warmed the hearts of the shipwrecked party, for these were their own countrymen, — brave fellows who pushed their little vessels into the farthest seas and feared nothing. The Professor and Henry grasped each hardy mariner by the hand and led the way to the Inspector's house, where the spokesman said he was George W. Dixon of Gloucester, Mass., and his schooner was the Rigel. A kayaker from Itivdlek had reached him with a letter, and, the wind failing, he had started immediately with a boat's crew for the long pull to Holsteinborg.

A consultation was now held, and the situation thoroughly discussed. Without a moment's parleying Captain Dixon agreed to render assistance, the only question being whether he ought to do so at once, thus breaking off his fishing trip with half a cargo, or complete his fishing and call at Sukkertoppen about the tenth of September. His crew were on shares, and he could not in fairness act without consulting them all.

It was decided that he should return to the Rigel and bring the matter before the men. If the schooner should come into the offing flying her flag on the following day it would be understood that Captain

Dixon would take the party back to Sukkertoppen at once and consult with Captain Barrett. Otherwise they might expect the Rigel at Sukkertoppen as soon as her cargo was complete.

The morning dawned bright, and with it came the Rigel. She stood in near the harbor and flew the Stars and Stripes. Preparations for departure were promptly begun, but one thing and another caused delay, and soon it was seen that they could not go on board until afternoon. In the meantime the natives, knowing that the strangers were about to leave, began to bring articles for trade. Among those which came to the boys were knitting needles and crochet hooks of reindeer bone or walrus ivory, a salt spoon and a mustard spoon of bone, a little ivory scoop or shovel, two pairs of slippers, a pair of kamiks, and a muff made from the pure white fur of the Arctic hare. This last was brought by one of the women, who accepted a white handkerchief, though usually the red or blue bandannas were preferred.

As Phil was walking up from the wharf with Inspector Müller, the latter made some remark about his belt and hunting-knife, adding, " Why do you wear a knife? There are no wild animals here in the town."

" That's true," Phil answered, " but it's useful — or was on our journey — for cutting meat and buttering bread."

" But you don't really need it, do you ? " asked the Inspector.

Phil could not be sure whether his questioner feared he might use the knife on a native in case of a quarrel, and so wished him not to carry it, or had simply taken a fancy to it and intended to find if he would part with it. The latter seemed the more reasonable supposition, especially since Mr. Müller had noticed it once or twice before and had asked to see it. So, thinking it would be but simple courtesy in view of the kind hospitality of his host, Phil stripped off both belt and knife and gave them to the Inspector.

" You 'll have to do some tight lacing, Mr. Müller," said he, " if you try to make that belt go around *your* waist," and with a smile he was dismissing the matter from his mind.

Not so the Inspector, who was genuinely pleased with the gift.

" My lad," said he, " you shall not give this to me without something in return."

Phil protested, but his friend insisted, and went into the house and brought out a beautifully carved paper-cutter of fine ivory, which Phil has ever since regarded as the choicest memento of his voyage to Greenland.

About the middle of the afternoon all was ready. After thanking their good friends of Holsteinborg for abundant kindnesses, the six said farewell and embarked in their boat with their Eskimos. Soon the Americans climbed to the schooner's deck, and their baggage quickly followed. But the faithful Huskies left them here. They had a dread of sailing in so large a vessel as the schooner, and preferred to return to Sukkertoppen in their own whaleboat.

15

CHAPTER XVIII

THE RIGEL OF GLOUCESTER

THE Rigel was a two-masted schooner of 107 tons' displacement. Her length was 89 feet, beam 23 feet, draught 13 feet, and she carried a crew of eighteen. She was built in 1889 after the usual Gloucester model, the main deck at the lowest point amidships being only three or four feet above the water, for convenience in launching and taking up the dories and heaving the fish and gear aboard. She was one of six American schooners fishing on the Greenland banks that year. Leaving Gloucester on the seventeenth of March, she had gone first to Iceland, but the halibut did not strike in very numerously there, so in July she had come to Greenland. Her capacity was about three hundred thousand pounds of fish, but she would never get so much as that in one trip. The ninety thousand pounds she then had was considered about half a cargo.

The relief party received a hearty welcome on board, the more so since, as Captain Dixon averred,

his crew had grown tired of looking at one another
so long. There is a monotony about protracted voyages very little appreciated by those who have never
been to sea. Especially is this true of fishing voyages with few opportunities of going ashore. On
the Iceland banks each American vessel has a particular crony in some one of the English fishing
steamers, and the interchange of social visits is
much enjoyed on both sides, but it was now two or
three months since the men of the Rigel had left the
Iceland fleet. They had read everything on board
that was readable again and again; they had heard
one another's yarns as often as they would bear re-
peating; and at last they had come to that stage
wherein they said only what had to be said, falling
into a kind of mechanical, humdrum existence.
Then it was that the advent of the little party,
with new ideas, new stories, new ways of life, became a godsend. Nevertheless it behooved the new-
comers to recognize the fact that a great deal of
generosity was also involved in their welcome. Every
one of these big-hearted sailors had voted to stop in
the midst of good fishing to come to their rescue.
For this the men would take no credit, simply saying
it was worth the uncaught half of the cargo just to
see faces other than their own, and never so much

as hinting at the nobler motive of humanity that had prompted their action.

" Just make yerselves to home," said they, heartily, and when night came they added, " Stow yerselves in any o' them bunks, lads, — it don't make no difference whose. We can sleep anywheres."

The wind being fair from the north, the Rigel was soon sailing at about nine knots toward Sukkertoppen. Up in the bows the little stove-pipe began to smoke furiously, hence the call to supper, when it came, was not entirely unexpected.

None of the six had ever eaten a meal in a schooner's forecastle. Room was made for them on the two converging benches, and the cook, a young and pleasant Southerner, placed the food on the triangular table before them, hot from the stove. Fried halibut and potatoes, white bread, biscuits, butterine, tea, and condensed milk, disappeared in great quantities, and the cook was kept busy filling up plates and cups.

The boys did not learn the names of all the crew, but, judging by appearances, they thought more than half of them were Americans. Captain Dixon's brother Will took charge of the vessel during such infrequent absences of the Skipper as his recent visit to Holsteinborg. The New Englanders all had intelligent faces, and indeed the crew as a whole was much above the average of the crew of the Viola in mental and moral quality. Of the foreigners, those whom they noticed particularly were two Nova Scotians, one tall and of French descent, known as Simon, the other shorter and with an accent that betokened a similar origin. There was also an Icelander who had been taken on during the trip and spoke no English.

Captain Dixon told his passengers that on the way to Holsteinborg from Nepisat (or Itivdlek) that morning the Rigel had bumped several times on a submerged reef, but came off without damage.

" I don't see," said the Professor, " how you dare to sail your vessel so close inshore on this uncharted coast. The regular harbors are bad enough, as we found out."

The Captain replied in words that showed the mettle of the American seaman. " Oh, we calculate to put her anywhere we want to go."

In the course of the conversation Ralph and Phil chanced to tell about the pole which they had found on the mountain, whereupon one of the crew remarked that it was left there by himself and a few others of the Rigel's men, who had climbed the peak a week before. They had placed the pole in an upright position and braced it with stones, but the big storm must have overthrown it.

The Rigel's party had found a den containing a family of blue foxes, but they had no means for smoking out the animals. Unquestionably the fox seen by the boys was a young one of that litter.

Captain Dixon told with what relish he had eaten dandelions gathered from the slopes. The Rigel's cook had served them up in appetizing style, " and," said the Skipper, " they tasted just like the greens we have at home." He smacked his lips at the remembrance.

" But what do you think of the Huskies ? " he continued. " Are n't they queer folks ? When they wanted something to eat they would come up and say ' scoffum,' and when they were looking to make a trade it was ' truckum.' They used to come to me with their pipes upside down in their mouths, and if I did n't take notice they 'd say ' smally tobac,' and they most gen'rally got it. They looked so comical I could n't resist 'em."

That night Professor Roth, Henry, and Ralph bunked in the cabin, while Malcolm, Andy, and Phil accepted the hospitality of the forecastle. Malcolm had the cook's bunk, and slept soundly amid the greasy coverlets, but his two young friends

were bitten by certain nocturnal insects not un-
common on shipboard, and thereafter they both
" sought the seclusion which the cabin grants."

By morning of the eighteenth the wind had shifted,
and the Rigel had to beat along the coast. About
mid-afternoon she was in the latitude of Old Sukkertoppen. A little later it was raining and blowing hard. The mainsail and jib were taken in, and
she ran under foresail, staysail, and a storm trysail
amidships. During the night the gale became a
severe sou'wester. All sail was taken in except a
reefed foresail, and the schooner lay to.

Toward noon of the nineteenth the wind fell off
and sail was added. The storm had stirred up the
vile-smelling bilge-water in the hold, and that odor
and the heavy sea together gave the boys their first
touch of seasickness. Their stomachs refused to
tolerate the stuffy little forecastle, and they had no
use for dinner that day.

On Monday, the twentieth, with a light head
wind, they beat down to Sukkertoppen, arriving off
the harbor early in the morning. It may well be
believed that the Professor and his companions
strained their eyes for the first sight of the Viola,
since, for all they knew, she might have sunk at her
moorings during their absence. But no; there she

was, in her accustomed place, and they could see
fully thirty kayaks putting out to meet them. These
were soon hovering about the Rigel as she drifted
in on the dying breeze. Two boats from the Viola
also came, bringing Captain Barrett, Captain Ayre,
and others.

"Bravo!" shouted Captain Ayre as they drew
near, and he waved his hat in token of his satisfaction with the result of the relief expedition. The
Captain of the Viola was equally pleased, and he
personally thanked each member of the party as
soon as he came on board. When the Rigel dropped
anchor alongside the Viola there were cheers and
the firing of guns, and everybody crowded to the
rail to see the trim little craft that had come to the
rescue. Caesar was so highly elated over the safe
return of Phil that words failed him, and he could
only say, "Bress yo', ma chile!"

As the exploring party from the Similik glacier
and the hunting party from Isortok Fiord had returned to the steamer on the previous day, negotiations were at once begun looking toward an
immediate departure from Sukkertoppen. The
captains and Danish officials held a conference, at
which Captain Dixon generously offered to take
everybody home free of charge after he had finished

his fishing. Delay was deemed impracticable, however, for the reason that provisions were already low. Articles of agreement were therefore drawn up, providing that the Rigel should forthwith convoy the Viola into port, and carry her passengers, for a stated sum to be paid by the owners of the steamer.

While these papers were being prepared, the natives came out with spears, paddles, and various trinkets to trade, and they found a lively demand. At length word was received that all hands except the Viola's crew should make ready to go aboard the Rigel, and that both vessels would set out on the homeward voyage together, and as soon as possible. Then all was confusion.

About one hundred tons of coal had already been taken ashore from the Viola to lighten her, — enough to supply Sukkertoppen for five years, — and now a few tons were transferred to the schooner, together with provisions and mattresses. From the schooner about fifty hundred weight of salt and some lumber were sent ashore and given to the Eskimos, since it was necessary to make room in the after-hold for sleeping quarters. Sixty trawl anchors and fifty-three trawl buoys were put on board the steamer for the same reason.

To each passenger, including the members of

Henry's party, was given a large dunnage-bag, which he was allowed to fill with his personal belongings, there being no room for trunks on the schooner. It was difficult to know what to take and what to leave. The boys, by Henry's advice, put into their bags such articles of clothing as were most needful. Then followed some of the Eskimo clothing which they desired to save, — such as the sealskin trousers, the eider-down cap, and the white muff of Arctic hare's fur. They decided to leave the kamiks, the slippers, the soapstone lamps, and most of the other small articles, as well as the spears and paddles, in their staterooms. Their rifles and shot-guns they cleaned and left also on the Viola.

When it came to the photographic apparatus, Phil was unable to decide at once. The pictures which he had taken up to the time of leaving Labrador he had sent home from Cape Charles, but he was fully as anxious for the safety of the hundred negatives which he had exposed with so much toil and painstaking along the Greenland coast. The likelihood that there would be opportunities for taking pictures on the schooner presently turned the scale in favor of keeping the camera and two boxes of unused plates by him. As to the negatives, which he hoped would preserve in concrete form the memories of Arctic scenes and people, he scarcely knew what disposition to make of them.

Mr. Dibb, the chief engineer of the Viola, of whom he inquired the chances of the steamer's pulling through, gave him little satisfaction. Nobody could tell, he said, how long the water-ballast tank would stand the strain that was now upon it. The steamer might gain the other side of Davis Strait and she might not. But Phil reasoned that as she had kept afloat for ten days without difficulty there was a good fighting chance of her lasting ten days more. Furthermore, if leaks occurred so that she could not be saved, there would doubtless be an opportunity to take off some of the more valuable goods. If he brought many boxes of negatives on board the Rigel they would be in the way, and very likely be damaged or destroyed sooner or later. So at last he left them all snugly stowed in the wooden box under the sofa in the stateroom. Many of his fellow-photographers who had brought plates came to the same decision, but those who used films were able to take their entire collections on board the Rigel without fear of breakage.

That evening a farewell reception was held at the Inspector's house, and many were the tokens of friendship and gratitude given to the hospitable

Danes by the Viola's passengers, one man presenting to the Inspector a very handsome Winchester rifle.

After an early breakfast on the Viola next morning, all except the steamer's crew and some of the cooks went aboard the Rigel. A small flock of sheep, which had been driven ashore when the Viola was abandoned in the ice and had been allowed to roam over a rocky island at Sukkertoppen, were now killed, with abundant assistance from the Eskimos, and taken upon the schooner to help out her supplies.

At the last moment Phil had a lucky impulse. Said he to Ralph, "I'm going to slip my ivory paper-cutter and those other trinkets from Holsteinborg into my pocket. They don't take up much room." Ralph and Andy and Malcolm decided to follow his example. Later, for reasons which we shall see, they were very glad that they made this decision.

CHAPTER XIX

ABANDONED AT SEA

ABOUT the middle of the morning, in a misty rain, the two vessels passed out of the harbor of Sukkertoppen, the passengers exchanging last words with the Danes, who had put out in the whaleboat among a great number of kayaks to witness the departure. Then "America" was sung, and various college cheers were given, until the little settlement and the harbor were lost to view behind a point of rock.

For the first few miles the Viola towed the Rigel alongside; then, after the Eskimo pilots had taken her well beyond the outmost rock, one end of the schooner's new and heavy cable, one hundred and fifty fathoms long, was made fast to the steamer's stern and the other end to the Rigel's bow, and the latter fell back to its full length. There was a moderate breeze from the south-southwest, and foresail and trysail were set that the Rigel might tow the more easily. While the sea was not rough, yet the rain and the heavy clouds furnished not the most auspicious conditions for beginning so critical a voyage, and Captain Ayre and Henry believed it would have been wiser to await clear skies and settled weather. But they had not now the responsibility of the decision.

Before long many of the passengers succumbed to that odor of bilge-water which had given the relief party qualms on the passage from Holsteinborg. Had it not been for this the cook could hardly have rested between meals, for only fifteen or so could be served in the forecastle at one time. Even as it was, but two meals a day could be prepared on the one little cook-stove.

Sleeping quarters were assigned early, and for a time everybody was busy getting mattresses and blankets in place, and stowing the dunnage-bags where they would serve for pillows. Those of the Rigel's men who had bunked in the cabin turned out of their quarters without a murmur and were crowded into the forecastle with the remainder of the crew, — all except the Skipper, who had to sleep within call of the man at the wheel. The cabin berths were then assigned to the college professors and elderly members of the expedition. They had the cabin stove for comfort, and it looked as if they would fare very well.

With cabin and forecastle filled, there remained for the twenty-five or thirty others the after-hold. This was just forward of the cabin, from which entrance was had by a low door. There was also a large hatchway at the forward end, which could be left open in pleasant weather. The dimensions of the after-hold were about twenty feet by fifteen, and the space from the deck-beams overhead to the coarse salt which partly filled it was only four feet. Upon this salt spare sails were spread, then the mattresses were arranged in rows close together, and here most of the passengers were to sleep for the next week or two, packed in like sardines. Henry and his companions placed their mattresses side by side in the starboard section and prepared to make the best of it. Caesar, at his own request, was detailed to help the cook, and found quarters in the forecastle.

"Dar ain't nuffin' ekal ter bein' busy, ter keep yo' sperits up," he said.

It was little wonder if the boys lay awake more or less that first night out. The sounds of sickness around them were not conducive to repose. They listened to the gurgle of the water on the other side of the planking and thought of the strange chain of circumstances which had brought them where

they were. Now and then they could distinctly feel
the tug of the Viola upon the cable, — a welcome
assurance that she was still seaworthy. But one
of the Rigel's men was constantly on the alert, axe
in hand, ready to cut the cable from the bow in
the emergency they all hoped would never arise.

All the next day the rain continued. At noon
the log showed 192 miles to their credit, and at a
favorable moment Captain Dixon shouted this fact
to Captain Barrett. The passengers grew joyful at
the prospect of crossing Davis Strait without mis-
hap. But as the afternoon wore on, a long swell
began to heave in from the south, and both vessels
rolled and labored in the trough. The Viola was
seen to be carrying her boats slung from the davits,
ready for instant lowering. By early evening the
wind had hauled more to the eastward, — that bad
quarter which had sent forth so many storms. A
few hours later it was blowing a fair-sized gale
and the seas were piling up, while the barometer
tended in the other direction. It was anything but
encouraging.

A little past midnight Phil was roused from
sleep by Ralph, who was sitting upright and putting on his coat.

" There's something wrong with the steamer,"

whispered Ralph, excitedly. "Let's go on deck."

While Phil groped for his coat there was hurried tramping on the deck over their heads, and they heard orders tersely given. Henry and Andy now awoke, and, perceiving that something unusual was taking place, they made ready to go' out with Ralph and Phil. By a lantern's dim light the four hastened to step over the prostrate figures of those who were still asleep, passed through the low door into the cabin, and thence up the short companionway to the after-deck. They found Captain Ayre and Malcolm there before them.

It was dark and cold, and raining. The wind had moderated slightly, but huge inky swells rolled up from the southward, blotting out the steamer's lights ever and anon. The Viola was showing a red light at her stern beside the usual white one, and they were told that she had been blowing triple whistles, — the signal agreed upon in case she should be in distress. Yet just before midnight her Newfoundland pilot had been heard to sing out, "She's good to go around the world in!" What had happened in the brief interval they could only conjecture as they stood on the slippery deck in the shelter of the trysail and watched the schooner's busy crew.

The Viola was towing slowly, but presently slackened till her consort had wallowed closer. Captain Barrett then hailed, " Stand by — we 're sinking! "

" Cut the cable and drop off in your boats, and we will pick you up," shouted Captain Dixon.

Faintly came the reply, " I will try to hold by the steamer till daybreak."

With that the Viola steamed slowly southward, heading into the seas.

A long hour of suspense wore by, then another, by which time gray daylight was displacing the gloom. All the passengers were awake and on deck now, and nobody thought of sleep. Once they saw black smoke pour from the steamer's stack and knew she was being coaled.

" The water is n't up to her fires, anyhow," said Henry, and the lads took hope that the leaks had been stopped.

" I don't see that she shows any signs of sinking," remarked Andy to the short Nova Scotian. But the latter thought otherwise.

" Oh, yes, she do," he replied. " I t'ink she be five feet down by der stern."

Andy appealed to Malcolm, who said he could not distinguish any change in her buoyancy, though she seemed to roll very heavily. It was impossible to see her at all except when both vessels were on the crests of the waves. When the watchers lost her stern lights they would keep anxious eyes on the lantern at her masthead; but sometimes even that went out of sight. Then they were breathless till it reappeared.

The dories nested forward were righted and provided with oars, and every preparation was made for launching them on short notice. Then there was nothing to do but await further developments.

At midnight the log had shown 289 miles covered since leaving the coast. That, with the southwesterly course, would put them near the centre of Davis Strait in the latitude of Cape Chidley, the northern point of Labrador. If the Viola could only hold out for two days more they could at least beach her on the Labrador side, and very likely save her with assistance from St. John's. At any rate they could take off the treasures she carried.

But at three o'clock or a little later, when the daylight was quite strong, somebody caught a glimpse of the first boat coming. She was tossed like a white cockle-shell on the big waves and made but slow progress. When she came alongside it was seen that she contained the stewards and cooks, with Second Mate Dahl in charge. No sooner was

she close in on the starboard quarter than all her
men, except the Mate and those at the oars, sprang
in nervous haste for the schooner's rail. Some as-
suredly would have missed and fallen had it not
been for the Rigel's crew, who spread themselves
along the rail and, catching one and all by the
hand or the leg or the coat-collar, tumbled them
inboard promiscuously.

While the boat returned to the steamer, a throng
gathered about the new-comers with eager questions.
The cooks reported that the Viola had sprung several leaks in the top of her water-ballast tank;
that one of the ship's boats, as it was being lowered
without orders by the panic-stricken firemen, had
been smashed to pieces against her iron hull; and
that an hour before midnight a stove had upset in
the second cabin and set the ship on fire, but the
flames had been subdued. That was the Viola's
second escape from fire, a pantry drawer having
burst into flames as she lay in the harbor of Sukkertoppen, when rats and matches were thought to
have been the cause.

The boat soon returned, bringing sailors' bags
and bedding. These were hustled on board so unceremoniously that one bag fell into the water,
whence Malcolm rescued it with a boat-hook. Mean-

time three of the Rigel's dories had been slipped into the water and sent to help take off the crew, and such provisions and light baggage as could be reached. The firemen and sailors were at length transported, and last of all, the officers. The carpenter, like many another shipwrecked mariner, took pains to save some of the choicest liquor in the steamer's wine-closet, but as he had stowed it all internally, he was anything but an able-bodied seaman when he arrived.

Captain Barrett saved the silverware, two chronometers, two sextants, the starboard and port lanterns, and some clothing, all of which were taken into the cabin except the lanterns. These, for lack of room, were left standing on the deck.

The sailors brought with them a cat, a canary-bird, and a puppy, which were their pets. They also picked up some small articles of the passengers' baggage before they left, and the fishermen brought off a number of satchels, cameras, and guns.

Phil watched in vain for any of his boxes of exposed plates, and his companions kept on the lookout for their rifles, shot-guns, and curiosities. It was impossible, in the hurry, to give directions to the sailors in regard to finding any particular object, and as strict orders were given that no passenger should attempt to put off to the steamer, each had to take his chances in the matter of salvage. Henry's rifle and Andy's shot-gun came in one of the dories, but nothing more belonging to their party. This was hardly to be wondered at, since the plates were under a sofa, the remainder of the hunting and fishing outfit was distributed in shadowed corners, and the Eskimo weapons were hung overhead. Gladly would Phil have let all else go if he could have saved the hundred negatives, on which were registered so much that could never be replaced; and Ralph mourned his collection of Arctic plants and blossoms. They were almost indignant when the last boat arrived with nothing but boxes of cigars.

Captain Barrett had cast off the cable before leaving, and the Rigel's crew were hauling it in and coiling it on the bow. Now that all was over, the passengers began to talk of the things that might have been saved had the sea not been so rough. The dentist declared that he could have found a twenty-dollar bill if he could only have gone to his stateroom. The official photographer had left three hundred dollars' worth of fine lenses on board the Viola and all his magnificent negatives. The scientists had lost a large collection of birdskins. A student, with supreme faith in the Viola, had taken almost nothing on board the Rigel except the clothes he wore, and those happened to be a suit of Eskimo clothing. He was already beginning to wonder what would happen when he struck civilization in that picturesque garb. There was no one who had not lost something, and it was a very dejected crowd of men who stood upon the Rigel's deck that dreary morning gazing across the wild billows. But there were no complaints. Personal safety was assured, and that was the main thing. "Thank God that matters are no worse," was the general sentiment.

More sail was now made on the Rigel, and soon the mist and rain blotted the unfortunate Viola from their sight. But they knew that not far off on that stormy sea she was still ploughing slowly ahead, the smoke curling from her stack, the lights still gleaming through her ports, — like a phantom ship that glides through the gale with no lookout on her bow, no hand at lever or wheel. For a half-hour perhaps she would move ahead, then, tossing at the mercy of wind and wave, she would gradually settle till the waters should make her their own. But no man saw the final plunge that took her to the bottom of the Strait.

CHAPTER XX

THE PUNCH BOWL

NINETY-THREE persons on a vessel only eighty-nine feet long! That was the state of affairs. Crowded before, they were now in the greatest straits for sleeping room. The Skipper opened up the main hatch and threw overboard about three hundred dollars' worth of trawl gear, bony line, and rigging, and an empty oil barrel. The members of the steamer's crew were then given the main hold in which to make themselves as comfortable as possible.

That evening the wind died out, and as the Rigel clambered over the big swells her foreboom slammed to and fro so violently that the sail had to be taken in until a light breeze sprang up from the southwest after midnight. By dawn the wind freshened again, hauling to west-northwest, and with it came more rain. The temperature was about 44°. During the afternoon there were glimpses of the sun, and the Skipper was able to determine his longitude.

It was weary work waiting for meal-time. Breakfast beginning at nine, dinner beginning at four, and a "mug-up" in the evening, — that was the best that could be done. In those who were not sick the hunger-pangs of a salt-sea appetite were strong by noon,— by four they were fairly famished. But if the cook, who worked night and day, never murmured, surely the others could not. Indeed he was the life of the forecastle, and by loudly proclaiming himself to be filling orders for every delicacy known to a Parisian chef, he kept the company in good humor while he dished out "salt horse" and halibut fins.

The boys took the earliest opportunity to obtain from one of the scientists the story of the exploration on the Similik glacier during their absence on the relief expedition. This professor and his companions had reached a small settlement called Ikamiut the first evening. They experienced much bad weather, but in the calm intervals they pushed up the fiord about eight miles to a spur of the inland ice. The mountains on each side of this fiord were about four thousand feet high. Four glaciers came down on the south side, the first within a thousand feet of the water, the second within five hundred feet, the next within three hundred feet, while the last projected into the fiord. At the east was a glacier from the inland ice, presenting a face-wall a mile in length and about three hundred feet high.

The party had ascended this great glacier six miles. From its front into the fiord icebergs were occasionally breaking away, and the detonations from this and other causes were so terrifying to the natives that they could hardly be induced to approach. When six miles back upon the ice the party had reached an altitude of eighteen hundred feet. They passed yawning crevasses, saw torrents gushing over the surface of the ice or plunging into holes, called "moulins," of unknown depth, and studied the medial moraines, or lines of stones and earth swept off from the "nunataks," or mountain peaks, which here and there pierced the ice-sheet. The glacier moved around these nunataks, dividing above them and closing again below. The rate of advance was found to be three or four feet daily. One of the nunataks rose two thousand feet above the surrounding ice.

While this scientific party was on the Similik glacier another professor had been making meteorological and geological observations at Sukkertoppen, the dentist had been studying the Eskimos' teeth, and a great deal of photography and collecting had gone forward. On board the Rigel there was much comparing of notes, writing up of diaries and journals, and dreaming of what might have been.

On the afternoon of the 26th of August the Rigel approached within half a mile of the largest iceberg any of the company had ever seen. No ice of any consequence had been sighted since leaving Sukkertoppen, the floes encountered on the northward voyage having been melted or dispersed; but this iceberg more than made recompense. It was a tremendous affair, rising from the water in a sheer wall which the wise ones judged to be fully three hundred feet high at its western pinnacle. On one shoulder of the berg a snow-field glistened in the sun. Southwest of the main pile, and probably joined to it under water, was a precipitous mass, perhaps a hundred and fifty feet high, with what looked like a navigable strait separating the two formations. Everywhere along the base of the ice-cliffs the white surf was gnawing, but for the present the monster seemed unconscious of its peril. With its grand peaks and headlands, its plateaus and cliffs and fiords, this iceberg resembled a model in marble of some bold coast, — perhaps that very coast in the far North which had launched it forth with mighty thunderings to brave the elements.

There was singing on the deck that evening by the college men, and others joined in until there was quite a chorus. After the concert the deepening darkness was partly dissipated by a blanket aurora which shimmered across the heavens and furnished a fine spectacle. Later came a thundershower.

It was late when our friends turned in, for there was little comfort in the crowded hold. They lay so close together that it was almost impossible to move, and their joints were invariably stiff and sore in the morning from keeping a single position so long. Some of the passengers could not even stretch out at full length, for men lay crosswise at their feet. Under these conditions it was amusing, when one man, who did not take kindly to hardship, complained because his nearest neighbors touched him. One of his companions, however, preferred not to be amused. Instead, he soundly berated the luckless offender for expecting to be favored when all alike suffered discomfort. The lecture was nothing less than artistic, and the boys listened with much amusement.

Two days later land was sighted bearing west-

The Rigel of Gloucester. (*See page* 224.)

"Crowded upon the deck of the Rigel." (*Page* 253.)

northwest, and Captain Dixon's observation showed it to be Spotted Island off the Labrador coast. As there were signs of bad weather early in the afternoon, it was deemed best to make the nearest harbor. A schooner was now seen ahead, and the Rigel was pointed so as to intercept her. She'proved to be the Minnie Mac of Halifax.

"Is there any harbor near?" hailed Captain Dixon.

"Yes," replied the other skipper as he sailed past, but he was so much impressed by the crowd on the Rigel's deck that he neglected to be very definite. Possibly he thought he was threatened by a crew of pirates. At any rate, before he passed out of earshot, his curiosity got the better of him, and he sang out, "For Heaven's sake, how did you get so many people aboard?"

"We have a steamer's crew," replied Captain Dixon, and ran up the American flag.

Other schooners were seen later, but too far away to be spoken. The whereabouts of the haven of refuge did not appear until a fisherman in an open boat close in toward the land was hailed and taken on board. He agreed to pilot the schooner into a little round harbor called the Punch Bowl for five dollars, and soon she was sailing in through an entrance known as "Victoria Tickle," only three hundred feet wide, between low, grassy hills. Before six o'clock she dropped her anchor in the very middle of the Punch Bowl, and apparently in the nick of time, for heavy clouds were moving across the sky and it was breezing up out of the southwest.

The dories were lowered at once and the Rigel's passengers hastened to go ashore, for they had now been cooped up a week with little chance to move about. The boys found that the scant fare and enforced inaction had weakened their muscles perceptibly, so that, in climbing the hill from the wharf walking was a burden, and running was almost impossible when they first attempted it.

There were only three dwellings here, and a mere handful of fishermen. The harbor indented an island, which, being small and bleak, was totally deserted in winter, the fisher-folk spending but six months in the place. Still two of the dwellings and several of the storehouses were very neatly built and painted. The third dwelling, evidently more ancient than the others, was a rude affair of weather-stained boards. The roof was covered with sods, and the chimney was a patchwork of wooden slabs which would certainly have caught fire in a drier climate.

Beside the Rigel, there were two vessels in the

harbor. One of these, the barkentine Violet of Bris-
tol, England, lay at the wharf and was loading with
cod for Mediterranean ports. The other was the
St. John's brigantine, Rose of Torridge. She was
anchored near the Rigel, apparently waiting her
turn.

The fishermen of Punch Bowl heard the adventures
of the new-comers with interest. Feeling sure that
the latter would welcome fresh food, they volunteered
the information that there were "bake apples"
somewhere over the brow of the hill. Even Ralph
did not know what "bake apples" were, but the
name was tempting, and a further hint that they
grew in the marshy places sent the lads and some
of the men off at once on the quest.

Beyond the hilltop the land fell away in rolling,
rocky stretches interspersed with swamps. For the
most part the latter were covered with grasses and
shrubs, and here the "bake apples" were soon discovered. They proved to be cloudberries, about as
large as a blackberry, having, when ripe, both the
color and flavor of baked apples. There were also
many curlewberries, small and round and very
dark.

After a feast of berries, the young explorers
returned to the Rigel, whose crew were engaged in

filling with fresh water the great cask on the deck forward of the cabin. This had been filled before leaving Greenland, and its contents had been freely used for several days for washing as well as drinking. It was soon seen, however, that the water must be husbanded, and strict orders had been given to use it for drinking only. There was now abundance again. The passengers could have wished for as good an opportunity to stock up the larder, for the mutton had given out a few days back, and, with the exception of codfish, no provisions could be bought here.

"Let's go out and catch some cod," suggested Phil, after supper. "That's more interesting than buying them."

"All right," said Andy, "I'm with you."

"Be careful to take an English boat," Malcolm advised. "It's against the law for an 'American or any foreign craft to fish along this coast."

Andy and Phil accordingly obtained a boat from one of the fishermen. As Malcolm had promised to go botanizing with Ralph, and Henry and Captain 'Ayre had been invited on board the Rose of Torridge, the services of Simon, the tall Nova Scotian, were enlisted, and they set sail for the harbor's mouth.

The wind was so strong that Simon was obliged

to row very vigorously on the port side. Even with that assistance it took all Andy's strength at the helm to hold the little sailboat to her course. Once they were almost blown upon a rocky point that threatened on their lee. Phil crouched in the bow in the shelter of the sail and resigned himself gracefully to whatever fortunes they might meet in thus navigating strange waters on a squally evening. They barely cleared the point, ran safely out through the Tickle, and heaved their stone anchor overboard a little way out from shore where the depth seemed favorable.

Simple Simon had his line down in a twinkling, and, pipe in mouth, appeared ready to catch a whale or anything that might come along. His fellow fishers followed suit as soon as their less experienced fingers could put the lines in order.

The first nibble came to Andy's credit. Of course they were not looking for exciting sport, since a cod makes so little objection to being drawn out of his natural element; but, as has been remarked, his weight furnishes a partial recompense for his sluggishness. Hence Andy grew rather elated to feel an unusually big fellow at the end of his line. He hauled with might and main, and was just wondering how to get him over the gunwale when he saw

17

that he had hooked up, not a cod at all, but a sizable rock from the bottom.

Neither of the others had any luck there, so the boat's position was changed somewhat. Finally Phil caught one cod of moderate dimensions, and as darkness was then coming on they had to be content with that. The anchor was drawn up by Simon and deposited in the boat, and the big fisherman was about to take his seat again when he uttered a shout of surprise.

" Look yonder, lads! " he cried. " Do ye see — just to wind'ard o' dat iceberg? "

This iceberg was one which had been near the northern horizon when the Rigel entered the harbor. It was a flat-topped berg and not particularly noticeable, and though it was now floating only a short distance to the northeast the boys had not given it much attention. They looked intently now, however, and could make out a small white object moving from the berg toward the land.

" It 's a bear! " declared Simon, " an' he 's comin' ashore! "

CHAPTER XXI

A POLAR BEAR

PHIL could hardly suppress his excitement as he watched the bear's progress landward. Andy, too, felt a sudden thrill of the hunting fever. As for Simon, he blew voluminous clouds of smoke at first, but presently forgot to puff, and his pipe went out.

" Oh! " sighed Phil, " if I only had my rifle here! "

" That's what you said when you saw the blue fox," remarked Andy.

" I know it. 'And I'm even worse off now, for I suppose the gun is at the bottom of the sea."

" Probably my shot-gun would n't be good for anything against a bear," said Andy, "but we might borrow Henry's rifle."

" It'll be dark afore ye can get it," said Simon, in a mildly dissenting tone, but he raised the sail nevertheless, and they began to beat back through the Tickle.

" I wonder if he saved any cartridges," said Andy, thoughtfully.

This was a momentous problem indeed, for a gun without ammunition was little better than no gun at all. Phil suggested that the Punch Bowl men might be able to help them out.

"I tell ye what, lads," cautioned Simon, "if ye want to shoot dat bear ye'd best not let too many in on der secret. Somebody else may rig up an' go off huntin'."

The wisdom of this remark was evident, and it was decided to consult only Henry and the others of their own party.

There was scant daylight left when the sailboat ran alongside the Rigel. Malcolm and Ralph were sitting on the schooner's rail and wished to know what luck. For answer Andy threw the solitary fish aboard the Rigel.

"Never mind," said Ralph. "They've bought a lot of cod while you were gone."

"Good!" said Phil. "Is Henry here?"

"No, he hasn't come back."

"Well, jump in here, fellows. We're going over to see him."

Ralph and Malcolm did not know why they should be invited on so simple an errand, but something in Phil's tone caused them to accept with alacrity, and the boat was then pushed off.

Captain Ayre had friends on the Rose of Torridge, and he and Henry had been listening to interesting yarns all the evening. They were quite ready, however, to come away when mysteriously summoned by the boys. The boat was now headed for the shore a little apart from the wharf, and Andy and Phil related in low tones what they had seen outside the harbor.

" A polar bear, eh ? " said Henry. " I did n't suppose they ever came so far south."

" Oh, yes," replied the Captain, " they drift down on the ice sometimes. One of the Cape Charles men told me they killed one there last winter, and that 's away south of here."

" We want to borrow your rifle, Henry," said Phil.

" What, youngster ? You two are n't going to hunt him all alone, are you ? "

" Why, yes; we can, can't we ? "

" What do you know about bear-hunting ? You 'd get all chewed up. Why, I understand there 's only one kind of bear that is considered more ferocious than the polar, and that 's the grizzly. They 're both ugly customers."

" Well, what shall we do, then ? "

" Let me see. I appreciate the fact that it belongs

to you to do the hunting, for you made the discovery
— you and Andy and Simon — ”

“ Der bear can go eat berries all day afore I
troubles him, sir,” broke in Simon.

“ Very well, then. Andy and Phil shall be the
Nimrods. But with their kind permission I will
borrow another rifle, and we’ll all go along as a
reserve force.”

This was perfectly agreeable to all concerned, and
as Henry had a few cartridges in his dunnage-bag
it only remained to determine the hour for starting.
Captain Dixon was taken into their confidence on
this point, since they did not know how soon he
planned to leave port. Upon his agreeing to await
the result of the hunt, either in the Punch Bowl or
at the mouth of the Tickle, four o’clock in the morning was named as the earliest practicable hour.

The boys had a rather restless night of it, and
were heartily glad when they saw the daylight growing. Caesar had been forewarned on the subject of
breakfast and had the meal in readiness. So quietly
had the preparations been made that though a number of the Rigel’s crew suspected something unusual,
none of the Viola’s sportsmen had the least idea of
what was going on.

“ I might’ly hopes yo’ won’t see no b’ar, Phil,”

was Caesar's parting word as the hunters rowed ashore, " but if yo' does, mind yo' see him 'fore he sees you, an' doan get nowhar near him."

The threatened gale had not materialized, and the day promised to be fair, with very little wind. The party took a course along the ridge which overlooked the Punch Bowl, Phil and Andy leading the way by common consent. Captain Ayre, Malcolm, Henry, and Ralph followed at a little distance, Henry carrying Captain Dixon's rifle. Simon had been urged to come too, but he had declined, not seeing that he could be of any service on a land expedition.

For over half a mile the walking was good, the top of the ridge being covered with short grass and small loose pieces of rock. There were no trees or even bushes to obscure the view, and had not the island's surface consisted of rolling hills and hollows, the hunters could probably have located their game before they were well away from the Punch Bowl. Where the ridge ended they paused to survey the visible parts of the land thoroughly before proceeding.

" A white bear ought to have some difficulty in keeping out of sight when there's no snow on the ground," said Henry. " I should think his instinct would have told him to stay on the iceberg."

"He was hungry, no doubt," said the Captain. "There are seals among the rocks, and berries in the marshes. Probably the land looked as attractive to him as it would have to us if we had sailed several hundred miles on a barren iceberg."

There was an extensive swamp between the end of the ridge and the rounded hill beyond, but Andy and Phil now plunged down into it regardless of the water, and the whole party were soon soaked to the knees. Having splashed through the strip of swamp, they climbed the slope, halting again at the top to see what the next hollow might offer. Their general direction was toward the east.

In this fashion they advanced for nearly an hour, the narrow Tickle being now on their right, while the land extended to the left a considerable distance. It was possible, of course, that the bear had gone around by the shore of the island, and might now be in the berry patches north of the settlement; and the farther Andy and Phil went the more did they fear that this was the case. They determined to proceed, however, clear to the eastern shore, if necessary, before exploring elsewhere.

Having met with nothing but disappointment thus far and being somewhat tired, their viligance was not what it had been. They fell to talking, **and** neglected to pause at the tops of the hills long enough for a thorough examination of the slopes and hollows before them. Hence it happened that as they passed over the brow of one of the eminences and down on the other side they were suddenly startled by a noise not far away to the right. A knoll partly cut off the view in that quarter, yet if they had been watchful they would have seen his bearship in time to have saved themselves by a well-directed shot. As it was, the bear, though also startled, collected himself much more promptly than the boys did. That he was both hungry and aggressive was quickly proven, for he made a rush straight for the intruders.

So sudden and unexpected was this onset that Phil, who was carrying the rifle, let it fall, and neither he nor Andy had time to pick it up. There was then only one thing to do, and they did it. They fled.

Curiously enough, all that Phil could think of as he ran was Caesar's late injunction not to go near the bear. Caesar was certainly wise. Proximity like the present was disconcerting, not to say unsafe. Phil knew now from experience. He wished he had taken Caesar's word for it.

The rear-guard, or reserve force, as Henry variously called it, was now two or three hundred yards behind. The precipitate retreat of the skirmishers back over that hilltop, closely pressed by what was undoubtedly the main body of the enemy, spread instant consternation in the ranks. Henry loaded his rifle in the first moment of alarm, but dared not fire for fear of hitting one of the boys. Captain Ayre and Malcolm drew their hunting-knives and prepared to close in desperately to the relief of the fleeing youths. Ralph had no knife and no gun, and could only stand and watch the terrible race.

Andy's first thought had been for the safety of his younger companion, and he had the courage and presence of mind to shout, " Run toward the others, Phil. I 'll run to the right. He can't follow us both."

This gave Phil a double advantage, for every step he took brought him nearer to assistance, while the bear was less likely to choose to pursue him than to continue after Andy. In fact this manoeuvre and the sight of the larger party caused the big animal to stop a moment on the crest of the hill. When he resumed Andy's trail the Nebraska boy had put fifty feet more between himself and the enemy.

Phil, though panic-stricken at first, was now himself again, and had no notion of deserting his friend. Being now relieved from immediate danger, he doubled on his tracks in order to regain the rifle. Reinforced by the weapon, he hastened in the direction taken by Andy and the bear, loading as he went.

Meantime Henry had found two opportunities to fire, — the first just as the animal started down the hill, and the second as soon as the rifle could be reloaded. In both instances the bear was in rapid motion, and so far as could be seen neither shot took effect. Andy was now being so rapidly overtaken that the nimble Malcolm, who was closely following, shouted, "Dodge him! Dodge him, Andy! Don't run straight!"

Andy had more than once been obliged to dodge a vicious bull on his father's farm, and had already determined that the same tactics alone would save him here; but he was glad of Malcolm's coaching, for he dared not look back too often. The ground was treacherous, and he needed to give all his attention to his speed. Upon hearing the warning he glanced quickly over his shoulder, saw that the time had come for the jump, and leaped to the right; but in doing so he failed to get firm footing. The shallow soil slipped beneath his foot, and he fell — fell so near to the bear's line of motion that the latter, as he went lumbering by, struck at him with his huge paw.

The boy felt a sharp sting in his leg and the tug of the claws in his clothing, and wrenching loose with all his force he rolled over and over into safety as the big animal's momentum carried him past.

This was Phil's chance to fire. The distance was considerable, but he seized the moment when the bear was turning and presented the whole side of his body. No sooner had his rifle spoken than the monster was seen to waver and stop.

" Bravo! " shouted the Captain. " That was a good one."

" Give him another like it," cried Ralph.

But before Phil could fire again, Henry had run forward to meet Andy, who, with his trouser-leg in tatters, and the blood streaming from a deep scratch, had jumped to his feet and was coming toward him with a celerity that showed he was by no means crippled. As they met, Henry pressed Captain Dixon's rifle into the lad's hands.

" You deserve to kill that bear, Andy," he said. " Now 's your chance."

Andy took the rifle, sank upon one knee to steady himself, for he was breathless with running, squinted along the barrel, and fired. That was the finisher.

The bear went down where he stood, and though he thrashed about for two or three minutes quite powerfully, he never rose again.

The whole party ran up with a shout, and examined the fallen game. He was a magnificent specimen, with a coat of long, fine fur. Three bullet-holes were found, one being a flesh wound in the back inflicted by Henry. It had not been serious enough to check the bear's career, and, as matters had turned out, Henry was well satisfied to have it so. The bullets fired by Phil and Andy had struck the spine and the heart respectively. Either would have been fatal eventually.

Andy's hurt was now carefully bound with a handkerchief. It was a painful scratch, but the lad made light of it.

At Henry's suggestion, and with the hearty approval of Andy and Phil, the Captain and Ralph, who, by force of circumstances, had little share in the battle, were constituted a committee to decide how the ownership of the bearskin should be determined. They accordingly withdrew and talked the matter over. At length they returned to the group seated about the bear, and the Captain reported.

" We find," said he, with as much gravity as if he had been the foreman of a jury, " that neither

Andy nor Phil has a superior claim over the other by reason of anything that has occurred since the bear was discovered. Your committee therefore decides that the question may be fairly settled between them by the toss of a penny. ` I hold the coin in my hand. Which of you will shout?"

" You, Andy," said Phil.

" No," said Andy, " I should feel better if you did it."

" All right. I 'm ready."

The Captain flipped the penny high in the air, and Phil cried " Tails! "

Ralph ran to the fallen coin. " It 's heads," said he. " Andy takes the bear."

Phil was the first to offer the hand of congratulation, which he did very sincerely. He felt that he owed his life to Andy.

The six now retraced their steps to the Punch Bowl, leaving the game temporarily where it was.

" The rear-guard did n't do much execution after all," mused Henry, as they discussed the morning's work. " Phil and Andy would have got out of the scrape without us."

" But just the same," said Phil, " when we ran back over that hill I was mighty glad there was a rear-guard, I can tell you! "

CHAPTER XXII

HENLEY HARBOR

THE tale which the hunting party had to tell aroused the greatest interest on board the Rigel, and all her company were eager to take a look at Andy's prize. There was not a ripple on the surface of the Punch Bowl, but Captain Dixon thought a spoonful of wind would be found outside if he could once get there, and he was not without resources for bringing this about. As the carcass of the bear lay not far from the Tickle, he promised that everybody should have a chance to visit the battlefield and without the necessity of walking through the swamps.

Three dories were now put over, and two of the crew were assigned to each. The dories were joined to one another tandem fashion, and the last of the three made fast a line from the schooner's bow. Then the six brawny fishermen began to row, not with the smooth, long swing of a college eight, but with a short and sturdy one better suited to the work in hand.

There were not wanting some on board the Rigel who said it could never be done. Strong as those oarsmen were, their efforts seemed puny when opposed to the inertia of so large a vessel. The first dory would tauten its line and yank the second boat ahead a little, and then the line would slacken. It was the same with the other connecting lines — they were taut for an instant only, and always slackened the next moment in spite of steady rowing. Usually when one was tense the other two were sagging. Yet a well-known principle in mechanics was presently illustrated. The power that was put forth with such apparent ineffectiveness was not lost. It began to tell upon the schooner. Her bow swung into line with the dories, and then a ripple showed that she was moving. In this manner, slowly but surely the Rigel passed out of the Punch Bowl.

As she approached the Tickle a fishing boat containing two or three men came alongside. One of these was a poor fellow afflicted with granular eyelids, which threatened to make him totally blind. He had heard, perhaps from the pilot, that there were physicians on the Rigel, and took this opportunity to get medical advice. The doctors examined the almost sightless eyes, and advised the sufferer to go to Dr. Grenfell's hospital at Battle Harbor for treatment. That was his only chance.

Between two and three hours of towing brought the Rigel opposite the point where the bear had been shot. The anchor was dropped, and all hands disembarked in the dories. Two stout poles and plenty of rope were brought along for use in transporting the huge beast to the schooner, and under Captain Ayre's direction preparations for this work were commenced at once. The ropes were made fast to the bear and to the poles in such a way that eight men could carry the burden, the poles passing along over their shoulders. As the bear must have weighed close to fifteen hundred pounds, the Rigel's men who volunteered for the task had each a fair load. Thanks to the abundance of expert instruction and assistance, the transportation was accomplished easily and quickly.

The towing of the schooner was then resumed, and she reached the mouth of the Tickle a half-hour later, where a breeze — a very light one — was found, as the Skipper had predicted. In the meantime, with the help of the Viola's official taxidermist, the bear was skinned by Andy in the centre of an interested ring of spectators.

What air there was blew from the south, and

hardly more than twenty miles were made all that day. It was almost as discouraging as waiting for the fog to rise from the .ice-floes on the northward voyage. But they had such diversions as watching the porpoises play beneath the bow, and buying cod from a fishing boat, and in the evening one of the professors read a story, and another described an adventure with Apache Indians near the Magdalena Mountains.

Had it not been for the bear and the cod, the food question would now have been serious indeed, for the larder was running low. The last of the sheep had disappeared some time before. Butterine and molasses were also gone, — the latter just as everybody had begun to crave it as the only sweetness in an otherwise very salt diet. Breakfast that day consisted of fish chowder, bread, crackers, and a choice of tea, coffee, or chocolate, — not a very filling bill-of-fare when the next meal, varied only by a strip of bear-steak in place of the chowder, came at four in the afternoon. But nobody grumbled. It was the best that it was possible to do. If any one still felt the pangs of hunger, he could fall back on the cook's imagination, and that never failed.

There was now a small measure of relief from the overcrowding in the main hold, since the chief mate of the Viola, the ice-pilot, the steward, and the second and third engineers — five in all — were left at the Punch Bowl at their own request. They intended to take the mail steamer for St. John's.

Nearly all the following day the Rigel lay becalmed in a dense fog on a green and glassy sea. The temperature of air and water, as noted by the scientists, coincided at 48°. Henry rowed out a little way into the fog and shot about forty birds, including gulls, jaegers, petrels, and guillemots. The skins he turned over to the taxidermist for mounting, but the bodies were handed to the cook and Caesar, who concocted a savory stew of them.

One more article of food gave out that day. This misfortune was due to the stokers, who stole an entire case of condensed milk and had consumed it all before the loss was discovered.

" A sneaking, dirty trick if there ever was one! " exclaimed Professor Roth. " That kind of conduct does n't shine very brightly alongside of that of the Rigel's crew. Those stokers don't seem to have the least sense of honor. The best I can say for them is that they may not all have been concerned in the theft."

The Skipper was also disgusted with those who

had stolen the milk, and he ordered that thereafter the stokers should be served last of all.

Owing to the fog a man was stationed on the bow whenever there was air enough to move the Rigel, and twice he gave the alarm. The first time it was an iceberg that loomed up ahead, and a collision was barely averted. The second time it was the sound of breakers roaring through the fog, and again the schooner tacked into safety. It seemed as if Captain Dixon had a wonderful sense of hearing at such times. Even when he had flung himself down on the salt in the hold for a snatch of sleep, let a cry be raised on deck and he was up and out before the others were aware of anything unusual. Between fog and ice and rocks and storms it was precious little rest that he could get. When every other space was occupied he would lie without a murmur on the hard cabin floor. In him heroism and generosity reached their well-nigh perfect ideal.

The last day of August found the voyagers close to Belle Isle, which they saw as soon as the fog lifted. This was the region of the Viola's early collision, and ten or a dozen large icebergs were even now drifting about here as if waiting for their prey.

In an interval of clear weather they passed and spoke a schooner bound to Green Bay, Newfoundland. Captain Dixon told the other the name of his vessel and asked him to report her with the Viola's party on board. This rather alarmed two or three newspaper correspondents who were hoping to send voluminous despatches as soon as they reached a wire. There was in consequence much speculation as to whether the other schooner or the Rigel would first connect with the rest of the world. Apparently the odds were much against the Rigel, and it seemed probable that the edge would be taken off the news before the newspaper men had a chance to send it.

The wind being contrary and fog and ice constantly threatening, it was decided to make a harbor again. The schooner was now within the entrance to the Strait of Belle Isle and a little to the south of Cape Charles Harbor. Henley Harbor, a few miles west within the strait, was the nearest port of refuge this time, and they sailed close in to find a pilot. Two men in a one-masted boat were hailed, and one of them agreed to take the Rigel in for four dollars, which was raised by what the Skipper called a " tarpaulin muster." This was the nautical of passing the hat.

Prominent in the coast-line as they approached was a huge flat-topped mass of basalt about two hundred feet high, known as the Devil's Dining Table. A similar elevation rose at the east to the same height, as if the two formations had been levelled by a single stroke of a gigantic plane.

Captain Dixon took the wheel in person, for the entrance appeared tortuous and beset by reefs. The pilot stood near, keeping a sharp watch and occasionally giving directions in a low tone. In the narrowest part a point of rock extended into the water on the port side, and all who were observing the navigation of the schooner looked for some word or signal from the pilot which would change the course to starboard. But though that person was evidently alert he said nothing, and the Rigel forged ahead straight for the rock. It was probable that the channel here was peculiar.

They had come within about fifty feet of the obstruction before the pilot acted. He then motioned quickly with his hand to turn the wheel to port. Clearly this was a mistake. The Rigel's steering gear worked in precisely the opposite way from that to which the fisherman had been accustomed. To throw the wheel to port would turn the bow to port, and they would be hopelessly entangled in two or three moments more. Yet Captain Dixon never faltered. The pilot was in charge and responsible. The wheel went over to port.

A precious second went by, and then another. And now at last the pilot noticed that something was wrong and turned in alarm. The Skipper was imperturbable, but for all that he appeared to be measuring with his keen eye the brief space that now separated the Rigel from the rock. Nobody thought he would actually run his vessel ashore, even if the pilot persisted in giving the wrong signal, but it was highly interesting just then to see how far he would go. Happily the pilot at this juncture made it plain that he desired the course changed to starboard immediately, and the Rigel swung round just in time.

The anchor was dropped about noon. A little store on the west side of the harbor first attracted the boys, and there they bought a supply of cheap candy, the best that was to be had. Captain Dixon negotiated for a barrel of herring, and Professor Roth secured molasses, oleomargarine, condensed milk, biscuits, and codfish.

Several humble houses nestled upon the rocks around the harbor, but the boys learned that only one family spent the winter here. As elsewhere along this coast there were no trees, but plenty of green grass flourished among the ledges.

A large party from the Rigel made bold to climb the Devil's Dining Table without so much as asking his Satanic Majesty's permission. To all appearances he was absent at the time, but near the southwest corner of the Table was a pile of rocks which, Henry declared, must represent the Devil's cook. These rocks presented a striking profile of an old lady with a funny little cap on the top of her head. Her hair was seemingly done up in a coil at the back, and this coil furnished a cushion for her head, which reclined at an angle of about forty-five degrees against a rock. Below and behind the head there was an open archway or hole large enough to contain two or three people. This hole served admirably to outline the back of the head and neck. The nose and forehead were excellent, the mouth was indicated by a dark groove, and two pointed rocks depending from the old lady's bosom looked for all the world like the ends of two ribbons. If the Devil were away, his cook was plainly asleep, so they left her undisturbed and set off to forage on the Dining Table.

It took some exploring to find a place where the rock could be scaled. For the most part it rose in a vertical cliff composed of five-sided columns similar to those of the Giant's Causeway in Ireland, and only where the formation was somewhat broken by a cleft could an ascent be made. Once upon the top, the climbers found it fairly level and covered with grasses and curlewberries, — not so fiery a diet as one might have looked for, considering the reputation of the absent owner. Along the edge of the cliff many initials had been cut by former visitors, but these could not long divert the eyes from the magnificent view of strait and coasts and bays.

So pleasant was it to have the freedom of the shore that all were loath to leave. Henry and his four younger companions roamed over to the east side of the Table, where, near a deep inlet, they discovered a sizable cave. Standing near its entrance and looking north Ralph noticed a fine human profile in the rocks, the eyes seeming to gaze intently out over the water. It was a region of wonders. On their return they found several outcroppings of the mineral known as Labradorite.

The finding of the cave suggested an outing that evening, and the five, after procuring a supply of fresh herrings and adding Captain Ayre and Caesar to their number, retraced their steps around the north end of the Table to the cave, in the entrance to which they built a fire of driftwood and cooked and ate the herrings, Phil imagining that they were castaways hidden in a safe retreat on some uncharted island.

That same night two of the professors took a boat and rowed to the headwaters of the harbor in search of a trout stream. They returned next morning with a good string, while one of the scientists, who explored in another direction, found an abundance of clams about two miles away.

Owing to fog, rain, and head winds, the first day of September was spent in port. In the evening the fisher-folk gave a dance on shore, attended by many of the Rigel's people. The latter nearly lost their way in the fog and gloom in going and returning.

The rain continued on the second, but as the wind had veered to the eastward Captain Dixon set sail early in the morning, and they passed out into the dark and stormy strait.

CHAPTER XXIII

A STRENUOUS NIGHT ON THE GULF OF ST. LAWRENCE

IT had been decided to make for Sydney, Cape Breton Island, rather than St. John's, hence the Rigel was headed westward. Hardly had they left Henley Harbor when they found themselves among icebergs once more. There were ten or fifteen of them dotting the strait, and very white and beautiful they looked against the dark-hued waters. But by the middle of the morning no more were seen. The Rigel had passed the utmost limit to which the incoming tide could carry them before it turned and swept them out to sea again.

As the waterway became narrower it was interesting to compare the shores of Newfoundland on the south with the coast of Labrador on the north. The Newfoundland side was green with grass and tall forest trees, while the Labrador coast was bleak and naked rock. In the interior of Labrador, beyond the scope of vision, there were forests as they knew, yet the strait was clearly a dividing line between two distinct climates.

The mists came down during the afternoon, and when they were thickest a steamer was discerned not far away to starboard, bound out. She was from Montreal doubtless, and going to England, — that is, if she should be so fortunate as to escape the icebergs out yonder in the mist.

Later the fog scaled, and a strong cold breeze sprang up which seemed almost frosty. Up the strait an outbound brig hove in sight, and, as she passed, several of her crew could be seen at work aloft in the teeth of the chill wind.

" I should n't want to be up there," commented Ralph. " I 'm cold in my overcoat down here on the deck."

" That 's nothing," said Malcolm, " compared with a sailor's work in winter. Why, these men on the Rigel will be out on the Grand Banks in the worst kind of weather and think nothing of it."

" And I suppose you and your father go out sealing while it is fairly cold in the spring ? "

" Yes; but then we are on a steamer, which is more comfortable," said Malcolm, modestly. " The square-rigged sailing vessels are the hardest to handle in winter, because they require the most work aloft.

You've probably noticed that the Rigel's sails are raised and lowered from the deck. The hard work on a fishing schooner is the fishing itself, and not the sailing, — except, of course, in very bad weather."

By evening the lighthouse that marks the western end of the Strait of Belle Isle was left astern, and the Rigel was fairly in the Gulf of St. Lawrence. The sea was becoming rough, but as it was Sunday a reverend professor, seasick though he was, managed to hold a service in the cabin after "mug-up." It was half a gale then out of the northeast, and there was a harp-like humming in the rigging. Jib and mainsail soon had to come down, and the trysail was set. The waves increased by leaps and bounds. Before long their crests broke over the deck, and once in a while a few bucketfuls of water splashed down through the cabin skylight, scattering the group around the stove. There was nothing for it but to batten down the main and after hatches, and make all snug for a disagreeable night.

Eventually the wind increased to a constant roar. At ten o'clock a rope started off on the foresail, and they hove to till repairs could be made, the decks getting well washed during the operation. The sail was then set with three reefs, and on they scudded. The boys concluded to turn in, though the chances

of sleep were not the brightest. Everything movable
was beginning to slide, including Phil's camera. To
get it out of the way he hung it, in its heavy box,
on a nail which projected over Andy's mattress from
a deck-beam three feet above. Andy regarded this
proceeding with some uneasiness, for the box swayed
violently and might fall. However, Phil thought
it would n't, and anyhow there was no other place;
so, without more ado, they rolled up their coats for
pillows in the dim lantern-light and crawled under
the blankets.

It was stuffy enough in the crowded hold, for the
hatchway was no longer open at the forward end
and there was very little air-space between the salt
and the deck. The only ventilation was by way of
the small door from the cabin, and as that compart-
ment was also full of men, what fresh air reached
the hold was well-nigh imperceptible. Then, too,
many in each place were very sick.

And how the Rigel rolled! She was a good sea-
boat, but that night she stood on her beam-ends every
few seconds. A passenger who usually slept at the
boys' feet had not yet come in, and thus they were
left free to slide. And slide they certainly did,
now to starboard, now to port, though they lay flat
on their backs.

As the evening wore on, complaints from the cabin were heard above the tones of the tempest and the rush and gurgle of waters along the planking. Somebody said the stove was getting too hot, and would n't somebody else put the fire out. Then there was a discussion as to the best means. It was suggested that salt might deaden it effectively, so Clarke, the handy man in the cabin, was directed to get a few shovelfuls from the hold. The boys heard him enter and fumble under the edge of the sail.

" I would n't wish to differ with the learned professors," said Malcolm, " but I have an idea that salt is n't the best thing to put into that stove. A' little water would do the business better."

Clarke had his orders, however, and whether he heard Malcolm's remark or not he soon had the fire covered deep. But with the fire half smothered, the passengers were likely to be wholly so, for the stove would not draw and the salt generated a dense, choking smoke which filled the cabin in a twinkling. From the cabin it came inevitably in through the little door, and those in the hold quickly changed their opinion as to the size of that door and the amount of atmosphere which could pass through it. Many were the groans and maledictions as the fumes began to permeate their quarters. Perhaps the sick were best off, for they were too miserable to care. But all were as nearly suffocated as they could be without losing consciousness, and a chorus of stifled shouts arose: " Put out that fire! " " Throw water on it! " " What blamed fool hatched that brilliant scheme ? "

But the author of the mischief was not fool enough to reveal his identity at any rate, and nobody was so uncomfortable as to prefer the cold deck and the risk of being washed overboard, so they all stuck to their places and passed as wretched a half-hour as could be imagined. By that time, the fire having been drowned out, the smoke became a little less troublesome, and the sufferers composed themselves once more to rest as well as might be.

Andy remembered dozing off several times, only to awake with a choking sensation. But at last he went fairly to sleep. Even then his rest was brief. He came to with a jump, conscious that he had been dealt an awful blow on the stomach and that he had exclaimed involuntarily " Ugh! " — very much after the manner of old Jacob, the pilot; after which, for some moments, he had no breath for further remarks (which may have been fortunate). He had come abruptly to a sitting posture, and the first thing he saw in the dimness was that camera tumbling over upon his legs. Probably he kicked it off upon Phil rather unceremoniously, for that youth also awoke, and asked with provoking innocence what was the matter.

"Matter!" As if it wasn't bad enough to be sliding about in a suffocating smoke without having a big box drop on your stomach as soon as you had managed to go to sleep, — and on an empty stomach at that! Poor boy! Perhaps it wouldn't have hurt so much — perhaps there would have been more resistance — if the last meal hadn't been eaten away back in the middle of the afternoon. But Phil calmed his good friend's troubled spirit by profuse apologies and genuine sympathy, and for the rest of the night the box was stowed somewhere down between their feet.

That same night one of the professors, a heavy man, was thrown across the cabin by a lurch of the vessel and badly bruised, fortunately escaping with no broken bones. He and Andy compared notes with mutual commiseration in the morning.

By daylight conditions began to better. The three reefs were shaken out of the foresail, and it was found that the Rigel could stand up under one. Two hours later the trysail and jib were set, and by noon the last reef came out of the foresail. As sea and wind diminished further, the rate of progress was maintained by canvas in inverse ratio. Mainsail and staysail were set by afternoon, and the breeze held throughout that night.

At daylight of September 4th Cape Anquilla was in sight, bearing south-southeast. The Gloucester schooner American, and several others whose crews were known to Captain Dixon, were spoken. A passenger recognized the skipper on one of these, having met him at Sidney, and sang out, " Cap'n McPhee! "

" Hello! " returned the skipper, who knew the voice. " Have you lost your ship? "

On receiving an affirmative answer he laughed loud and long. It was just what he had predicted of an expedition that would take an iron ship to the far North. As he asked no further explanation he must have taken it for granted that the Viola had been put out of commission by the ice.

Since Captain McPhee had not heard of the disaster, the correspondents took fresh hope that the schooner going to Green Bay had not yet reported, or at least that the news had not reached St. John's and the cable. Their eagerness to be at Sydney that evening in time to wire the morning papers was now increased tenfold, but the wind disobligingly fell off that afternoon upon the approach of a rainstorm, and little sailing could be done for some hours. Not until early the next morning in a light head wind did the Rigel beat up into Sydney Harbor.

CHAPTER XXIV

HOMEWARD ON THE PORTIA

THE first man to come on board the Rigel was a runner for a cheap boarding-house. He said no news had been received concerning the loss of the Viola. The correspondents therefore wasted no time in getting over to the telegraph office, where they filed lengthy despatches for the New York evening papers.

"They'll have the news all over the country by night," said Henry. "Even Andy's family ought to hear it by to-morrow morning at latest. I imagine our friends have passed some anxious hours since they read our letters from Cape Charles."

"I should just like to see Mother's expression of countenance when she reads to-night's paper!" exclaimed Phil. "She'll be tickled to death."

"I dunno 'bout dat," said Caesar. "I 'se mightily drawn ter b'lieve dat she'll survive de speunce ob de readin' ef she ain' died ob anxiety befo'hand.

It am gwine ter be a happy day fer dis yere ole man when he hands yo' ober ter de Missus alive an' kickin'.''

This speech brought down the house, and Phil declared he fully appreciated Caesar's watchfulness and sage advice.

While Captain Dixon was busy with the custom-house officers a committee of the passengers went over to South Sydney and arranged for a banquet at Colonel Granger's Sydney Hotel that evening. Everybody went there later in the day on the steamer Peerless. In the short time that was available the room had been decorated with American and British flags, and those of two or three universities. With what heartiness the seafarers fell to work upon the oyster patties, chicken croquettes, salad, sirloin of beef, roast lamb, plum pudding, ice-cream, etc., may easily be imagined. The waiters must have thought they had eaten nothing for a fortnight, which was n't so far out of the way as it might have been. But that night they rejoiced in an abundance of good things, and vain regrets for the Viola were laughed away. After the feast came speeches by Captain Barrett, Captain Dixon, Professor Roth, and others of the Viola's people; and Henry, in response to repeated calls, spoke briefly for the little party whose work had made the rescue possible.

Many farewells were said next morning, for about half of the passengers were to return to their homes from this point by train, while most of the others, including our camping party, intended to accept the generous offer of the owners of the Viola to fetch any or all of the shipwrecked ones home on a sister ship, the Portia, plying between St. John's, Halifax, and New York. Captain Dixon was ready to take all hands to Gloucester on the Rigel, but there were few for whom sailing had not temporarily lost its charms.

Those who were to return by the Portia were to embark for Halifax by the steamer St. Pierre at half-past three that afternoon, and at that hour Henry and his companions took leave of their good friends, Captain Ayre and Malcolm, who were soon to start for St. John's by another steamer. They parted with mutual respect and good wishes.

It was a day's voyage to Halifax, and the Portia was then at her wharf. She was to leave for New York the following morning, so the campers had an opportunity to visit the citadel and the public gardens. They were interested to find New York papers containing the despatches sent from Sydney, and had the satisfaction of knowing just what their friends had read about them.

The Portia was somewhat crowded, and Ralph and Phil were obliged to sleep on sofas; but this was luxury after the hold of the Rigel. In her navigation of Newfoundland waters this steamer had met with some thrilling experiences, one of which was so remarkable as to be without a single parallel. Henry heard something about it and asked one of the officers for the story when they were at table.

" You probably know well," said the officer, " that it is considered dangerous for a steamer to pass close to an iceberg. There may be projecting masses beneath the surface of the sea, or a portion of the berg may break loose and overwhelm the ship. The vibration of sound or the swash from the bows of a passing vessel may even cause a berg to collapse utterly.

" Well, sir, the Portia was steaming along the Newfoundland coast a dozen years or more ago in the near vicinity of a large iceberg, though it was supposed that the interval separating the ship from the berg was a safe one. Suddenly, to the consternation of all on the Portia's deck, it was seen that some change had taken place in the ice-mass, and presently up from the depths directly under us we saw a great greenish bulk of ice rising to the surface.

" There was no time to do anything. Before the helm could act or the engines be stopped the huge submerged fragment — a berg in itself — reached the steamer's keel. When I saw that ice below us you may well believe, sir, that I never expected to set foot on the dry land again. It seemed certain that the Portia was doomed. Up came the ice and up went the steamer bodily out of the water, with her propeller whizzing around like mad. Then a strange thing occurred. It happened to be an inclined plane upon which the Portia rested. No sooner was she stranded high and dry than she began to slip back, helped by a big wave which washed over the ice, and almost before we could realize it she had ridden into the water again as jauntily as if she were just launching from the ways. Yes, sir, — a fact. She left a trail of paint on the ice, but beyond that she was as good as ever."

An uneventful day of steady progress followed, but at night the Portia anchored in a fog off Pollock Rip lightship, while whistles, horns, and bells, frequently heard, revealed the presence of an unseen fleet, mist-bound like herself.

Monday, the tenth, also brought much fog, though, after proceeding, they occasionally ran into a few miles of clear weather and could see the shores of Martha's Vineyard. The fog here was noticeably drier and whiter and less transparent than the fogs of the far North. The latter soaked into the clothing and fell in drops from the rigging, even when it was possible to see through it to a considerable distance; but this southern fog blew over and around in soft white masses, which hardly dampened anything, though dangerously opaque.

During almost every clear interval sailing vessels were in view, and it could not be doubted that many more were concealed in the alternate banks of mist. But the Portia halted not. Blowing her whistle when there was need, she rushed at full speed through fog and sunshine alike, and when some one ventured to ask one of the officers if there were no danger of striking some craft in these much travelled waters, the answer was, " We never have."

When the steamer was about five miles off Cuttyhunk Light a thick bank of fog was entered. The passengers were at luncheon in the saloon, and Henry and his young friends were deep in reminiscences, when suddenly the engine-bells rang. To the great majority of the passengers this meant nothing, but

those who had been on the Viola had grown super-
sensitive to that sound. Coming when the fog was
dense it was equivalent in their minds to a warning of imminent danger, and this interpretation was
confirmed the next instant when they heard the
rattle of the chains and felt the lurch to starboard
as the wheel was thrown hard over. The engines
were reversed at the same moment, and the propeller set up a mighty throbbing as it struggled to
grip the yielding brine.

It could only be in vain. They were sure of that.
The fog was too thick and the speed of the Portia
too great. If anything had been sighted directly
ahead she must strike it. The chief officer at the
head of the table, and Henry and the three lads,
looked silently at one another and waited for the
crash.

It came after a moment of sickening suspense,
with a horrible sound of splintering timbers. There
was no perceptible jar to the Portia, but her headway was lost as by some heavy, though movable,
obstruction. All sounds of conversation and laughter ceased instantly and utterly in the dining cabin,
to be succeeded after a momentary hush by awe-
struck whispers, cries of alarm, and stern voices of
men. The mate, without a word, sprang up and

made for his post. Henry, who sat next, followed as far as the head of the companionway, but halted there, for in front of him stood two ladies — Spanish or Italian he judged them by their dark eyes and rich olive complexions — presenting such a picture as would make the fortunes of any two actresses who could reproduce it. Their pose, their expression, their gestures, were those of absolute terror and hopelessness. They wrung their hands and lifted their eyes to Heaven, moaning that all was lost and they would die. So intense and pitiable was the mental anguish they were suffering that Henry stopped to speak a word of reassurance.

No sooner did he speak than both besought him to save them, and clung to his arm. They were trembling, and so pale with fright that he feared they would swoon. When the door on the port side behind them swung to with a bang they were completely unnerved, and screamed, thinking some new calamity was upon them.

It took several moments to calm his charges, for Henry could hardly convince them that they were safe, even for the time being. Meantime the other passengers were thronging up past them and out upon the deck, some with breakneck haste, others more deliberately and calling for order. Andy and

Ralph and Phil were borne along in the rush, but kept their wits about them. Henry, as soon as he had restored some degree of confidence to the ladies, passed out also by the starboard doorway, through which he had already caught a glimpse of wreck and ruin.

CHAPTER XXV

THE WRECK OF THE DORA M. FRENCH

THE scene that met Henry's eyes as he emerged beggars description. A large three-masted schooner lay alongside, but separated from the steamer by an interval just sufficient to prevent passage from either vessel to the other. The schooner's bow was even then settling beneath the waves close to the bow of the Portia, while the stern rose high. Forward of the wheelhouse the Portia's deck was a mass of wreckage. The schooner's bowsprit, foremast, and foresail lay there all tangled up with the forestays and foretopmast of the Portia, and both rails were crushed and twisted for a considerable distance. Evidently the schooner had been struck close to or a little forward of her foremast and had well-nigh been cut through. It must have gone hard with any of her crew who chanced to be in the forecastle.

Plainly the doomed craft was sinking fast. She was held to the steamer by the tangle of rigging forward, and the broken spars were creaking and groaning as the two vessels, straining apart, rose and fell with the waves. The second officer had been upon the bridge at the moment of collision, but the captain was there now, giving hasty orders to lower away the boats. Already the crew were working at two or three of them, and judging that they would be more of a hindrance than a help, Ralph and Phil and Andy kept clear of their operations. Every second was precious now. It was a race with Death.

While most of the crew were thus occupied, Captain Barrett of the lost Viola was doing the work of a dozen men. He was in no wise responsible for this disaster, nor for the handling of the crew, and the consequent sense of freedom seemed to give him the strength and energy of a giant. He seized an axe and began to clear away the wreckage. Already the Portia was listed to starboard. The great wire stays lying across her decks threatened to act like the arms of an octopus and drag her down with the schooner. Captain Barrett hacked them in two with ponderous blows and never stopped till he had severed, with some help from the crew, everything — wire, hemp, or wood — that could possibly bind the vessels together. By that time the axe was about as dull at one end as at the other.

Meanwhile the passengers, including the boys, had crowded to the rail and were watching the schooner in a kind of helpless fascination. Before their eyes was being enacted the most exciting struggle for life that they had ever witnessed. Of the schooner's men two only could be seen. They were working to clear away a boat which swung at the starboard side near the stern, and as they worked, the water was creeping, creeping, up the deck toward them. They heeded it not, but pulled and jerked the ropes and seemed to accomplish nothing. Would they never get that boat into the water? What could be the matter?

The one who appeared to be the skipper, a middle-aged man dressed in blue, suddenly left his work and rushed into the cabin. The other, as if disheartened or dazed, sat down upon the stern-rail. In a moment the skipper returned with an axe and began cutting away the refractory ropes. It was too late.

" Jump! Jump! " shouted some of the Portia's people, but it was doubtful if they heard.

Hardly had the axe swung twice before the stern of the schooner was swallowed up with all that was upon it, and a great inrushing whirl of waters covered the spot. Even strong men turned away sick at heart, but the same fascination drew their eyes back to the troubled surface of the sea, where now a little jet of steam came up. It was from the cabin stove. Still the spectators, shuddering and breathless, hoped against hope for some sign of life.

" There! Look there! " cried one.

The man who had sat upon the rail as the schooner went down had come to the surface and was striking out bravely. Captain Barrett, in twenty places at once, ran into the cabin for life-buoys. These he threw as far out as he could, but they fell far short. The swimmer, beside, was headed the other way. But now fresh hope arose, for around the Portia's stern came the first of her boats, lowered from the farther side. She contained three men, one being Henry, whose absence the boys, in their excitement, had hardly noticed.

But what of the schooner's captain? They try to pierce the depths where the foam and bubbles have cleared for a moment. Ah, he too is coming up! See! Under the water he is swimming feebly. Courage! Can he do it? A few strokes more!

But it is not to be. Even as he rises almost to the air, consciousness departs, his arms cease from their motion, and the eddies that still whirl about the spot draw him down. He rises no more. The

Sea has claimed another sailor as she has claimed many and many a one before, and up there on the coast of Maine the widow and the fatherless will look in vain for his home-coming.

There is only the mate in sight now, and he is making a splendid fight. He has struggled out of the suction and grasps a splintered timber. It gives him scant support, and he lets it go. He tears at the neckband of his shirt that is almost strangling him, but it is too stout to break. Now he comes to the cabin-door and puts his arms over it, cheered by the excited people on the Portia. But the man's weight and an inopportune wave turn the door over, and he loses his hold. Now he looks despairingly at a floating barrel. It is too far away for his failing strength. A piece of topmast offers a better chance, and he strikes out for it. Soon he reaches and flings his arms over it. That is likely to bear him up, thank Heaven! And now the boat is closing in upon the spar. The rowers draw in their oars. Carefully they reach out and grasp the half-drowned man, and as he is firmly pulled up into safety he falls senseless into the bottom of the boat. He does not hear the cheer that breaks again from the throng on the Portia, but it does not matter. He is saved.

20

While this was being accomplished a few of the crew were lowering the starboard lifeboat. The little craft that had rendered such prompt service was not one of the regularly numbered boats. She had been slung above the lifeboat on the port side away from the wreck, but proved the handiest in the emergency. With the starboard lifeboat, near as it was to the scene of disaster, delay after delay occurred. The blocks were found to be unhooked, the plug was out of the bottom, and much of the space needed for the oarsmen was occupied by life preservers. When she finally swung out from the davits it was a motley crew which jumped into her. Perhaps one-half were seamen of the Portia, but the others were volunteer passengers, at least one of whom was intoxicated and probably sought his own safety. Andy decided that he could be of assistance here, and he leaped in and seized an oar.

As soon as this boat was pulled away from the steamer she began to fill, owing to the absence of the plug, and the second mate, who was in charge, had all he could do to get to the spot where the schooner sank. She had to be bailed constantly, and at last, when the water in her was deepening, the mate guided her back and informed the captain of her condition. The latter ordered her kept out on the search, and the order was obeyed. She cruised awhile about the maintopmast, which with a part of the sail remained unsubmerged, and poked among the floating spars and boards; but it was too late for further rescues. She was still out when a large schooner loomed out of the fog to starboard and rounded the Portia's stern. She must have been following the lost vessel at no great distance. Having read the steamer's name, she tacked and stood away toward the land as if to report the disaster.

The sole survivor, as soon as he had recovered consciousness, gave his name as Jem Murphy, and said that he lived in New York. He was fitted out with dry clothes and taken to the smoking-room to recuperate. There he stated that the lost vessel was the Dora M. French, hailing from Bangor and bound from Hoboken to Boston with coal. Her skipper was Captain French of Lincolnville, Maine. The steward, familiarly called Sims, came from Bucksport. Of the other two men the mate knew very little. One was called Harry, and one Tom. The former had told him that he had been a member of the crew of Mr. Vanderbilt's steam-yacht Alva. Until the mate recovered consciousness he had supposed that all his companions had been picked up, and was greatly surprised to learn that he alone had escaped.

There was a persistent rumor among the passengers that a second member of the schooner's crew had climbed aboard the Portia among the wreckage forward, but upon investigation it was determined that the man they had seen was a seaman of the steamer, who had gone there to ascertain the damage. So far as the Portia was concerned, this consisted of a ragged hole at the water-line near the stem, the loss of the foretopmast, and a general wreckage of rails and rigging forward. A bulkhead had prevented the water from reaching other compartments, and the steamer was in no danger.

Andy, splashed with the salt water, soon rejoined Ralph and Phil. "It's queer," said he, "but all I can think of when I look down on that wreckage is this:

> 'Ask of the winds that far around
> With fragments strewed the sea.'

Where did I ever hear that?"

"Why," said Phil, "that's from the poem Casabianca that used to be in our school reader."

"Sure enough. 'The boy stood on the burning deck,' — that's what it is. I had n't thought of it for years, but somehow that sea all covered with splinters and spars set it a-going through my head. I'm sorry for those poor fellows who went down.

Four, was n't it? We did n't see any of them from our boat."

"The mate says he saw one of them swept overboard by a spar when we struck," said Ralph. "I 'm sure two must have been below decks."

"The worst of it all is," observed Henry, "that it was one of those accidents that never would have happened if ordinary precautions had been taken. What's done can't be helped now. The time to have helped it was beforehand."

For a half-hour or more the Portia remained near the scene. Then she proceeded for New York, and, strange to say, she continued at full speed again through the fog. In view of what had taken place this seemed the height of folly. Every moment the passengers expected to see another vessel in their path, — possibly a steamer, which could give as well as take a death-blow.

Toward evening, to the relief of all, the fog cleared away with a change of wind and a lively thunder 'shower. No one would have been greatly surprised if the Portia had been struck by lightning. Indeed any accident seemed possible to the boys, and even probable, after such a summer of calamities. But the lightning flashed harmlessly around them. Off Little Gull Island the Portia took a pilot and next morning, the 11th of September, came safely into her berth.

" I'se brought him back all safe, Missus Schuyler," said Caesar, hat in hand, as Phil kissed his mother, " but dar was times when I war pow'ful 'fraid I could n't! "

THE END

RESH, HEALTHY BOOK OF T-OF-DOOR ADVENTURE

ld Seeking

on the

alton Trail

NG THE ADVENTURES TWO NEW ENGLAND S IN ALASKA AND THE THWEST TERRITORY

By

RTHUR R. THOMPSON

Illustrated. 12mo. Decorated cloth, $1.50

e best presentation that we have had of life in londike. — *New York Times.*

good story that will interest every boy. . . . is not only a new setting for a tale of adven- but a certain amount of instruction in an tive form. — *New York Tribune.*

New Books for the Young

THE OAK-TREE FAIRY BOOK

Edited by CLIFTON JOHNSON. With eleven full-page plates and seventy-five smaller illustrations from pictures by Willard Bonte. Crown 8vo. Decorated cloth, $1.75.

HERE are the old favorites in a version especially suited for the home fireside. The interest, the charm, and all the sweetness have been retained; but savagery, distressing details, and excessive pathos have been dropped. Its clean text combined with its beautiful illustrations make it the most delightful collection of fairy tales ever published.

BOYS WHO BECAME FAMOUS MEN

Stories of the Childhood of Poets, Artists, and Musicians. By HARRIET PEARL SKINNER. Illustrated by Sears Gallagher. 12mo. Decorated cloth, $1.25.

INCIDENTS in the childhood of eight celebrated men — poets, artists, and musicians — are here wrought into stories that are interesting for the story's sake. Essentially the incidents are true, and thus the book is in a measure biographical; but the stories are told with so much animation and color as to make them as interesting as fiction.

FRENCH PATHFINDERS IN NORTH AMERICA

By WILLIAM HENRY JOHNSON, author of "The World's Discoverers," "Pioneer Spaniards in North America," etc. Illustrated. 12mo. Decorated cloth, $1.50.

A GRAPHIC and comprehensive narrative of French explorations. It recounts the adventures and discoveries of such men as Cartier, Champlain, Marquette, La Salle, etc. Written in a direct and forceful style, especially adapted for younger readers, with the historic facts stated accurately and clearly, this book is at once interesting and instructive from beginning to end. The great value of the book lies in the fact that it presents the whole story of French exploration from the beginning.

ND - #0121 - 220223 - C0 - 229/152/19 - PB - 9781331382423 - Gloss Lamination